BLACKOUTS AND BREAKDOWNS

BY

MARK BRENNAN ROSENBERG

Copyright © 2010
Newcomer Press

All rights reserved. No part of this book may be reproduced in any form or by any means without the prior written permission of the publisher.

Printed February 2010

ISBN: 978-0-9817424-1-0

Custom Print Now / Newcomer Press
10015 Old Columbia Road
Suite B-215
Columbia, MD 21046
410-312-5581

Cover Design by: Cameron Northey

I happily dedicate this book to:
All My Children's Erica Kane.

Watching you bed every man in Pine Valley and looking so damn good doing it, is an inspiration to me and made me the man I am today.

TABLE OF CONTENTS

Introduction	7
Chapter One: SHIT SHOW	9
Chapter Two: THE TRUTH ABOUT THE BABY JESUS	15
Chapter Three: I'M COMIN' OUT!	27
Chapter Four: THE PICK-UP ARTIST	45
Chapter Five: HOW TO TURN A STRAIGHT MAN GAY IN UNDER TWENTY MINUTES	63
Chapter Six: BOILING POINT	75
Chapter Seven: HAPPY NEW YEAR!	85
Chapter Eight: GREETINGS FROM OUR NATIONS C(R)APITOL!!!	91
Chapter Nine: MY SUPER EX-BOYFRIENDS	129
Chapter Ten: ADVENTURES IN SOBRIETY	175
Chapter Eleven: BABY DADDY	231

INTRODUCTION

Imagine a summer filled with fabulous trips to the beach, weekend excursions to the mountains and a fabulous group of friends that hung on your every word. Imagine having a successful doctor as a boyfriend and having the best sex of your life. Imagine if you will, living in a world without any consequences and having the time of your life. Now imagine, not remembering half of it. By the summer of 2008, my drinking had taken on a life of its own. I was constantly partying and carrying on, while ignoring the important aspects of my life. I felt I had tried to make it work in D.C., where I was living at the time, but the two of us were simply not a fit. I am a New Yorker after all, and as far as I am concerned, there is nowhere else to live. I had moved to D.C. on a whim and after less than a year, I was done. My real friends were in New York and I knew if I had just put forth a little more effort, I would be back where I belonged, living the life I had always imagined I would lead. But the truth was, I had more than enough time and plenty of opportunities to have that life and ended up pissing it away either by making bad decisions or conducting inappropriate behavior wherever I went. I had all but given up any dream of returning to New York. I would talk about moving back, and take an occasional interview, but I was not putting forth the effort required to make a happy life for myself. I was twenty-five years old, waiting tables and not doing much to become the respected adult that I thought I deserved to be. My life had turned into a constant bar crawl, hopping from bar to bar, flirting with acquaintances and making false promises to myself, and everyone around me. The only thing I began looking forward to was having that first drink. But one drink always led to many and in a short time it became clear to everyone around me that a problem was brewing, literally.

SHIT SHOW

I was only seven years old when my parents divorced. At the time, I was devastated, thinking their choice to separate was going to ruin my life. Looking back on it, it was most likely the best possible choice for everyone involved. They hated each other so much, had they stayed together for the remainder of my childhood, someone would have ended up dead or even worse, paralyzed. They had knock down drag out fights where chairs were thrown, obscenities flew out of their mouths and someone always ended up hysterically sobbing in a corner crying for their mother. That someone was usually my father. Both of my parents have huge personalities and they were just not a good fit. As a child who grew up watching far too much daytime television where fights such as these were prevalent, I did not really understand what the big deal was. It wasn't until I was discussing the night that my mother hurled a place setting at my father's head, over a snack pack on the playground with my friend Brian, that I realized these were not normal dinnertime activities.

"But on *One Life to Live*, when Gabrielle slapped Max in the face after she found out he had an affair, all was forgiven. But the shit really hit the fan when Gabrielle found out she was pregnant with Max's baby," I said as I swung back and forth with the remains of pudding all over my face.

"What's an affair?" my friend Brian asked.

"I think it's like when you share your lunch with another girl or something," I responded.

< 10 > BLACKOUTS AND BREAKDOWNS

"Oh," Brian said, "I don't think my parents fight like that." Brian's parents did not seem like real people to me. His father was the local weatherman and came on my TV right before Erica Kane. I always asked him if they knew each other, but he insisted they didn't.

"My parents fight like they do on TV. So it must be OK, right?" Brian and I concluded that behavior like that was in fact normal and proceeded to smack any girl that came across our path that day. After getting detention I realized that throwing things at people was not OK whether they did it on television or at home.

Shortly after my parents separated was when the real dramatics began. Custody hearings, claims of adultery, unscrupulous affairs, surprise weddings, trips to exotic locales and the occasional surprise witness on the stand of a trial were everyday occurrences in the Rosenberg household. I did not even need to tune into my favorite daytime dramas because my home was where the real action was.

After some time, things began to calm down a bit. My father eventually married a horrible woman name Joyce, whose main role in everyone's life was to make it as difficult as possible. She was my personal arch nemesis. She was the Brooke English to my Erica Kane. She forced my father to relocate to Baltimore of all places, and since my parents had joint custody, once a week and every other weekend, my little brother Kevin and I were forced to trek up to Baltimore from D.C. to visit my father and his whore of a wife. It was fun at first, but every Monday night my mother would drive us to Columbia, Maryland (a half-way point between Baltimore and Washington D.C.) and drop us off. Then our father would pick us up and drive us the rest of the way to Baltimore. Since we were still children, and had to go to school, my father would then drive us the next day from Baltimore back to D.C. at six in the morning for school.

It was a miserable existence. At age ten, I was already addicted to coffee because there was no other way for me to make it through a sixteen-hour day without it. Every other Tuesday, my brother and I would rise at a quarter to six in the morning, drive to D.C., go to school, participate in our after school activities and then go to daycare where our mother would then pick us up and we would have a family dinner. Our weekly trips through scenic Maryland were fun for a while, but they quickly became draining. My little brother would flat out fall asleep during school and by mid-morning I would get the shakes from caffeine withdrawal. Something had to be done.

"I have a brilliant idea!" my father proclaimed on one of our infamous trips to Baltimore. "Tonight, you will sleep in your school clothes for tomorrow. I will have your lunches packed and you can eat breakfast in the car. I have also mapped out an entirely new route to school that will save us exactly fifteen minutes. But we can't stop on the way. There will be no bathroom breaks, so if you have to take a shit, you are just going to have to hold it. I bet your whore of a mother could not have come up with a plan like that!"

My ten year old face looked at my father as he was driving his Jeep up Route 95 towards Baltimore and replied, "my whore of a mother probably wouldn't have made her children get up at the ass crack of dawn to go to school just so she could prove a point."

"Don't say ass, and don't call your mother a whore," my father replied.

"But you…"

"I am allowed to call your mother a whore – you are not."

My father's brilliant plan worked for a few weeks. Aside from our clothes being wrinkled everyday due to the fact that we slept in them the night before and my brother getting two cavities because he bypassed brushing his teeth altogether, things were going as planned until one morning, when my father's plan completely backfired.

We were on our way to D.C. one Tuesday morning and all was well. My father popped the cast recording of *Guys and Dolls* into the tape player and we were all singing along. We had just recently seen the revival of the show on Broadway and the three of us would sing all of the lyrics to every song and it would occupy our time between cities. Amazingly, I was the only one in that car who turned out gay. However, midway through our trip, when I was getting ready to belt out my big solo number, *Adelaide's Lament*, I noticed that my brother was totally forgetting that he was supposed to be providing my back-up.

"Kevin, what the hell is wrong with you?" I yelled, "When I say, 'le drip, le drip, the post nasal drip', is when you come in to back me up. How many times have we rehearsed this?"

"Sorry," my brother said.

"Dad, rewind the tape. We are going to do this until Kevin can get it right," I was a bossy little queen, even then. "I just don't understand it Kevin, this is what we do every single Tuesday morning. You know your part, now fucking do it. Dad is Nathan Detroit, I am Adelaide and you are back up for Nicely Nicely when we do the big *Guys and Dolls* finale, Jesus!"

All of the sudden, my brother let out a wail like nothing I had ever heard before. He began screaming at the top of his lungs. My father panicked. Not knowing what to do he turned his head around to see what my brother was screaming about. However, when he turned his head around, he also turned the steering wheel with it. Before he knew it, his Jeep was swerving out of control. He tried to steer it back in the right direction but before he could, he crashed into a tree. He grasped me with a soccer mom death grip and the airbags exploded into the front seat of the car. My father panicked, but everyone inside the car was in one piece. After gathering his bearings, he turned around to see my brother still crying hysterically.

"WHAT THE FUCK IS WRONG WITH YOU?" My father screamed into the back seat of the car.

"I JUST SHIT MY PANTS!!!" my brother screamed at the top of his lungs.

"What?" my father asked again.

"I. SHIT," breath, sob, "MY. PAAAAAAAANNNNNNNNNTTT TSSSS!!!!!!"

Not knowing what to do, I began laughing hysterically until my father knocked me upside the head.

"Why didn't you just ask me to stop the car?" my father asked.

"BEEEECCCCCAAAAUUUUSEEEEEE!" my brother was hysterical. I had never seen him like this before. Aside from the time that he found my mother putting Christmas presents out under the tree one year even thought she explained to him that she was just "Santa's Helper".

"What the fuck is wrong with you?" my father asked.

"You – told – us -- we couldn't" -- sob, sob, sob, deep breath, "pull the car over to stop to go to the bathroom. If we did, it would make us late."

I laughed, "looks like we are going to be late anyway." I was then smacked upside the head again.

"If it's an emergency we can always stop," my father said.

"But you hate to be late. That's why we have to sleep in our school clothes every night," Kevin replied.

My father's face went lax. It was as if he could finally see the toll all of this was taking on us. The fighting, the early morning car trips, the custody battles. He knew just the person who was to blame. He picked up his Zack Morris style car phone and dialed.

"God damn it Pat!" he yelled into the phone as my mother picked up, "get your ass over to the school and bring Kevin some clothes. He just shit his pants and he is going to need a change of clothes."

"God damn it Keith!" my mother yelled back into the phone.

"God damn it Pat, this is all your fault!" my father said. They continued to bicker for an hour while my brother sat in his shit filled pants and I tried to salvage the cast recording of *Guys and Dolls* from the tape player.

My father drove his wrecked Jeep to school and my mother dropped off clothes for my brother. My brother's shame has since been restored but that was the last time we visited my father during the week.

THE TRUTH ABOUT THE BABY JESUS

Nancy Reagan was right. Marijuana is the gateway drug. Even though she had stolen Ronald Reagan away from my beloved Jane Wyman, star of the greatest show ever on television, *Falcon Crest,* Nancy hit the nail right on the head when she told everyone to say no to drugs. But when you are in high school and everyone else is doing it, it just seems like the thing to do. Had I just said "no", it would have saved me a lot of time experimenting with drugs in college while I was trying to "find myself." I have heard very few people have found themselves while they are face down in a pile of cocaine, but that's just me. Needless to say, my high school years were filled with smoking weed and carrying on like a complete moron.

I first attempted to smoke weed with my friend Maureen, who I had known for quite a few years. She invited a few of our friends over to her house for a "pow-wow." We were all going to smoke weed out of a peace pipe and get to know each other better. The first time I smoked, I didn't feel much, but sure enough, after a few more tries, I was high as a kite. I loved the feeling of getting high. It was as if nothing else in the world was going on when you were high. You're just floating on a cloud, watching everything go by in slow motion. A few months after I first tried smoking, I was a full-fledged pothead. I would skip class during the day and drive around with Maureen and the rest of our friends and get high and eat a lot of junk food. It was a great way to spend the last few months of high school and since I had already managed to get into a good university, I didn't really care anymore. Life was good for now and I was going to enjoy it before adulthood really began.

My best friend in high school was Evelyn. She was a Russian Jew, who had dark skin and everyone always assumed she was a Mexican or half white and half black, but she was just plain old Russian Evelyn. Evelyn was a little more conservative than I was. She did not always take the chances that I took and always thought long and hard about what her next move in life was going to be. I was a free spirit and just went along with whatever seemed fun at the time. But Evelyn would always chime in and let me know what the difference between right and wrong was and that I was usually making the wrong decision. The two of us had been inseparable in high school. We did pretty much everything together and I truly loved her as a fag-hag. She, of course, did not know she was a fag-hag at the time, but she was a little heavier theatre geek and I was her scrawny ABBA loving soap opera fan. If that isn't a fag/fag-hag relationship than I don't know what is. The two of us had befriended Stephanie Buck, who was a blonde airhead with a heart of gold and the three of us were like the three musketeers. The three musketeers who; were high most of the time. Our last year of high school was spent smoking weed, singing ABBA and show-tunes and driving around causing trouble wherever we went.

One night before Christmas of our senior year of high school, Evelyn and I were driving around, smoking a blunt, waiting to pick up Stephanie from a family dinner. Somewhere along the way, we made a wrong turn and Evelyn and I found ourselves lost.

"Where the hell are we?" Evelyn asked.

"Doe Lane," I replied.

"Doe?"

"Yea, as in a deer, a female deer."

"Oh, gotcha," she replied. Of course, we had to bring it back to musical theatre. We drove around but still could not figure out where we were. Evelyn made another right turn, this time onto Buck Lane.

"Look Evelyn," I said. "We're on Buck Lane. Wouldn't it be funny if Stephanie lived on Buck Lane. Then she would be Stephanie Buck of Buck Lane. Ha, ha, ha," I laughed as if what I had said was the funniest thing she had ever heard. It wasn't. Shortly after, we found Stephanie's house and entered. All of her family had been there for a holiday dinner and everyone was pretty loaded.

"Hey Stephanie," I said looking like Cheech. "Did you know there is a street called Buck Lane?"

"No shit," Stephanie replied. "That's awesome."

"Yea, it's right around the corner."

Stephanie's uncle who had had about fourteen too many cocktails overheard our conversation and chimed in: "Stephanie, go steal the Buck Lane sign and bring it back to the house."

"What? Uncle Pete, you're crazy," Stephanie replied. I, on the other hand, thought this was an amazing idea.

"Come on Stephanie, let's go steal the Buck Lane sign. It will be funny."

"I don't know about that guys. What if we get arrested?" Evelyn, the ruiner of everyone's fun said.

"No one is going to get arrested," I said. "Don't worry. It will be fun."

Stephanie, Evelyn and I grabbed some tools out of Stephanie's garage and got in the car in hopes of stealing the Buck Lane sign. We drove back to Buck Lane and parked the car.

< 18 > BLACKOUTS AND BREAKDOWNS

"Ok Mark, get the sign," Stephanie said.

"Why do I have to steal the sign? My last name isn't Buck," I replied.

"Because it was your idea jackass," Evelyn replied.

Evelyn and Stephanie sat in the car as I climbed on top of it, tools in hand, ready to pry the sign off of its hinges. Shortly after I got on top of the car, I realized that it was Stephanie's drunken uncle's idea to steal the Buck Lane sign, not mine, but I was already on top of the car so I just continued. I used the wrench to try and unhinge the sign, but it would not budge. I then tried to use the hammer we had brought to hammer it off, but that did not work. I had never used either a wrench or a hammer before in my life and was not really sure what I was supposed to do. I banged on the sign with the hammer a few more times but nothing happened. I climbed off the car and got back inside.

"I can't get it off," I said, "It won't budge."

"I guess we are going to have to forget about it then," Evelyn said.

"No!" I yelled. "I am getting the Buck Lane sign if it's the last thing I do." I was now determined to steal this sign. I gathered myself and got back on top of the car, tools in hand, ready to get the sign. The livelihood of the Buck family depended on it. I hammered away at the sign again but nothing happened. I used the wrench to try and unscrew the sign from the pole it was on, but nothing happened. It was dead-bolted and wasn't going anywhere. I got back into the car.

"I don't understand why you are so determined to get this f-ing sign," Evelyn exclaimed.

"Because you have put this idea in my head now and I want it!" I replied. The truth was, I really did not care, but I was high enough and the idea was in my head so as far as I was concerned, it was the only thing on my agenda for the rest of the evening.

"Cars keep coming by and looking at you standing on top of our car trying to steal this sign. Maybe this isn't the best idea after all," Stephanie chimed in.

"Whatever, bitches. Drive down the street so I can try and steal the other Buck Lane sign," I said.

Evelyn drove down the street to where the other Buck Lane sign was located. Again, I got on top of the car and tried to rig the sign off of its latches to no avail. I got back in and felt totally defeated. I had the thought of stealing this sign in my head and nothing would make it go away.

"Oh well," Stephanie sighed. "Maybe it wasn't meant to be." Evelyn started the car and we drove away from the Buck Lane sign. As we drove down the street, I could not help but notice everyone's lawns were decorated quite nicely with Christmas decorations. Suddenly, as I continued smoking a blunt, I had an epiphany.

"Evelyn, stop the car!" I yelled. Evelyn's car came to a complete stop. "Fuck the Buck Lane sign, let's steal Christmas decorations off of people's yards."

"Oh, Mark I don't know about that," Evelyn said, "What if we get caught?"

"We won't get caught. It will be fun. Let's drive around and try to steal decorations. It will be hilarious."

It took a few minutes, but I finally convinced the girls that it was the most brilliant idea I had ever had. We had smoked a lot of weed and anything from an impromptu trip to New York or opening up a brothel would have sounded like a good idea. Evelyn drove down the street and we pulled up to a house that had a full on cardboard cutout nativity scene on their lawn.

"I bet I can steal the Baby Jesus," I said.

"I think that's sacrilegious. Isn't it?" Stephanie asked.

"I think it's pretty much like slapping God in the face or something," Evelyn said.

"Whatever," I replied as I hopped out of the car. I crept onto the lawn of the unsuspecting family's home. They had a full on nativity scene going on, complete with animals and wise men, but it was the manger with the Baby Jesus that I had my eye on. I crept closer to the scene and saw that the family was sitting in their home, around a piano singing Christmas carols. All of a sudden, I was literally the Grinch who stole Christmas. I crept over a wise man and around the sheep, keeping one eye on the family inside to make sure they could not see what I was doing. As I made my way around the nativity scene, I knocked over the Virgin Mary. Thinking I had little time, I left her there and made a break for the Baby J. He looked so cute lying in the hay. I grabbed him and ran back to Evelyn's car. I could hear Evelyn and Stephanie laughing uproariously as I made a beeline back to the vehicle. I hopped in and Evelyn sped away, laughing all the way.

"Oh my God, that was the funniest thing I have ever seen!" Evelyn said as she high-tailed it down the road.

"I have never laughed so hard," Stephanie replied. "I want to try. Let's find another nativity scene."

"This time, get a light up Baby Jesus," I said. "My Baby Jesus wants a brother!"

We could not find another nativity scene until we passed a church.

"Is it bad to steal from a church?" I asked.

"Yes!" Evelyn and Stephanie said in unison.

I, however, convinced Stephanie that it was not, in fact stealing, but borrowing as we could always return him. I told her that if she took the Baby Jesus from the church, we could give it back and say that we stole it because we were doing research for school. She somehow bought it and got out of the car to steal the other Baby Jesus. She went up to the nativity scene and tried to steal it, but this was a light up Baby Jesus and there were cords involved. Stephanie ran back to the car in a fury.

"I think there was a nun or something in the bushes. I heard some rustling." Stephanie said as she got back into the car.

"Stephanie, I don't think nuns hang out in bushes. I think they fly or something," I replied.

"There were cords. The Baby Jesus was connected to Joseph and so on. I could not untangle them. It is going to take a few minutes to get everything unconnected."

"Whatever Stephanie, let's try another one." I said.

Evelyn drove around as we looked for another Baby Jesus to steal, but there were not many around, as we must have wandered into a Jewish neighborhood. Finally, I decided that we needed to ditch the Baby Jesus idea and just start taking whatever we could find. There was a treasure-trove of Christmas decorations that were ripe for the taking. Evelyn pulled up to a home that had a black Santa Claus on its lawn.

"Oh my God, I want that for my bedroom!" I said as I got out of the car. I had in fact always wanted a Black light up Santa Claus for my room but was too shy to buy one for myself so I figured I might as well just steal one. I crept onto the lawn where the Black Santa was surrounded by reindeer and looking extra jolly. I unplugged him from his outlet and brought him back into the car. Again, Evelyn and Stephanie were giggling like schoolgirls as they watched in awe as I stole the black Santa from his home. When I got back into the car, black Santa in tow, I decided his name was going to be Jerome. That night Evelyn, Stephanie and I had not only stolen a Baby Jesus and Black Santa, but a light-up Frosty the Snowman, garland off of someone's fence, ornaments off of trees, Christmas lights, a potted planter that looked like a swan that had nothing to do with Christmas but we thought it would be fun to steal anyway and a huge cardboard snowflake.

It was like we had gotten a high off of all of the goods we had stolen off of people's yards. Not knowing what to do with all of our merchandise, as our parents were sure to question where it all came from, I decided to leave it at the Starbucks that I worked at for safe keeping. I was one of the managers at the time, so I had a key and let myself in to drop off the goods. I scattered my goods throughout the Starbucks, leaving the Baby Jesus right by the cash register so everyone could bask in his glory as they were paying for their coffee.

The next morning, my co-workers were stunned to see my loot throughout Starbucks but thought it was hilarious nonetheless. In fact, they thought it was so funny that someone drew a cup of coffee in the hand of the cardboard cutout of Baby Jesus and wrote "God Bless Starbucks" underneath it. Everybody loved the Baby J. He was like our new mascot.

That evening, Stephanie, Evelyn and I met again, with full intentions for stealing a light up Baby Jesus. We got into Evelyn's car, smoked a few joints and were on our way. We drove around the suburbs looking for a light up Baby Jesus. Since the employees of Starbucks had defiled our cardboard Baby Jesus, we had to move on and find something that would last forever. Our thievery had bonded the three of us and we were as thick as thieves now, literally. We drove around but could not find a light up baby Jesus. I resolved that we should go back to the church we had gone to the night before and try to steal the baby Jesus from there.

Evelyn pulled up to the church. All was quiet as I hopped out of the car on ready for my mission. I crept onto the lawn of the church looking for any nuns that may be hiding out in the bushes. Baby Jesus was in eyeshot and I made a beeline for the nativity scene. Once I got there, I could see why Stephanie had so much trouble the night before. There were cords everywhere and navigating where each cord went was like making your way through a labyrinth. I managed to find the outlet, unplugged the Baby Jesus, grabbed the cord, and tossed the Baby J under my arm and ran back to Evelyn's car. When I got into the car, Evelyn and Stephanie were laughing so hard, I thought they were going to throw-up.

"Oh my God!" Evelyn said through her laughter, "that was the funniest thing I have ever seen."

Stephanie was laughing so hard that she could not even speak.

"It was like you were carrying the Baby Jesus…" Evelyn continued laughing hysterically, "like…" she was laughing so hard, I didn't know if she was still breathing, "a FOOTBALL!" She finally cried. I don't know if she thought it was funny because it was a Baby Jesus I had under my arm or that fact that it was the closest I had ever come to actually looking like I had ever played a sport.

The three of us sat in Evelyn's car and laughed hysterically for the next few minutes. Happy with my latest conquest, I put the Baby Jesus on my dining room table and told my family that he was going to be our centerpiece for Christmas dinner that year. A few days later, Evelyn called me and told me to pick up the town newspaper because she thought I would get a kick out of it.

I went to the corner and picked up the newspaper. I flipped through it until I got to the section where the headline read: "THE TRUTH ABOUT THE MISSING BABY JESUS." My mouth dropped. I had finally made it into the newspaper, except, no one knew it was I who had stolen the Baby Jesus. The article chronicled the night that the Baby Jesus went missing from the local church and what they thought happened. They even had a reward for anyone who knew his whereabouts. Thinking my cheap brother might turn me in for cash, I knew I was going to have to put the Baby Jesus into seclusion. I laughed because I thought it was funny, but the people at the church were outraged by what had happened. Evelyn, Stephanie and I decided never to steal again, but that Christmas was one of the most magical times of my life.

Where Are They Now?

The Baby Jesus – The Baby J and I had a long lasting relationship. He came to New York with me, when I moved up there. He stayed with me in every apartment I moved to until his light bulb blew out, almost causing a small fire. I ended up throwing him away.

The Black Santa – My little brother Kevin took care of the Black Santa for many years until he went to college and it was destroyed at a keg party.

The Potted Swan – The potted swan enjoyed a long career in my front yard, until it too was stolen, possibly by its rightful owners.

Frosty – Frosty enjoyed a long holiday career of entertaining the children on my father's front yard. When my father realized he was Jewish, he threw Frosty away.

Evelyn – Evelyn lives in Astoria, Queens in a building that is always decorated with Virgin Mary's and Baby Jesus' come Christmas time. I have tried stealing them on several occasions, but she will never let that happen.

Stephanie – Stephanie now lives in Tampa and I think she is bisexual.

I'M COMIN' OUT!

"Are you gay yet?" Jason asked me as I approached him on the corner of 72nd Street and Park Avenue. I had just moved to New York a few days before and Jason knew it was only a matter of time before I would come out of the closet. We had, after all, performed a medley of the songs of George M. Cohan together in high school chorus so I knew that he would not be surprised if I told him I was gay.

"Not yet," I replied and then realized I meant to say "no." Jason smiled at me. "I know when I do come out of the closet that I definitely do not want to be outed at a T.G.I.Friday's like you were." A few years earlier, our friend Valerie outed Jason in front of all of our friends at a T.G.I.Friday's after rehearsal for a show we were doing at the time.

"Ha," Jason laughed, "next time we are eating at a Bennigan's, I will make sure that I let Valerie's mother know what a huge vagina enthusiast she is." We walked down the street and spoke about what our first days of college were like. Jason and I had been friends for a while in D.C., where we grew up and then moved to New York at the same time. I admired Jason because he was who he was and made no apologies for it. He was outed at a chain restaurant in Bethesda, Maryland, in front of a group of his peers and took it in stride. Nothing ever fazed him, but things were different in New York. I knew it was only a matter of time, before I joined Jason as an out homosexual, but I figured day four was a bit too early to come out and I was nervous about what the repercussions might be. Pretty much everyone in New York seemed gay, so I knew I would fit in immediately. I had moved to New York to go to school, but I also moved there to be myself. I was tired of

D.C. and the way everyone always pretended to be something that they were not. I knew in New York, I could be whoever I wanted to be and would be accepted. As Jason and I discussed dorm life and how much we loved going to school in New York, he convinced me to go to a gay bar in the West Village where one of his friends from school was working.

"I don't know if I want to go to a gay bar," I said.

"Oh, whatever Mark. You are queerer than a three dollar bill," Jason replied. "Just come. It does not mean that you are gay if you hang out in a gay bar. It will be fun."

Jason and I made our way down to the piano bar in the West Village. On the way, we passed a Ruby Tuesdays and although I was hungry, we did not stop to eat, as I was afraid Jason would out me. Once at the piano bar, I realized it was like nothing I had ever seen in my life. The bar was in the basement of a building and was pretty dingy looking. Inside the bar, gay men of every age, stood around a piano singing show-tunes and having a gay old time. Everyone seemed so comfortable with themselves and everyone looked like they were having a great time. Jason and I walked in and Jason went directly to the bar.

"I'll have a Jack and Coke," he said. Jason, just barely out of high school and not old enough to legally buy cigarettes at this point, was given his drink as I watched in awe. "What do you want?" he asked me.

"Uh," I was trying to think of something exotic to drink. I was playing with the grown ups now and needed to order something a little fancy. "I'll have a whisky sour, with lots of cherries."

The bartender winked at me and gave me my drink and bypassed looking at my fake ID. I was so excited to be in a gay bar, drinking and singing show-tunes. This was pretty much what I had imagined gay life in New York to be and I was thrilled to know that my dreams had actually come true. I loved how sophisticated everyone looked with cocktails in their hands and now I looked high-class too. I had only drank in secret before, hiding it from my parents at parties, and now, I felt like a true grown up. The glamour of it all amazed me and the allure of finally being who I knew I always wanted to be was right at my fingertips. But there was no way I was coming out tonight. Jason and I had a wonderful night, singing show-tunes and making new friends. Jason told me that the following night he was going to meet up with a guy named Chris for a date. Jason met Chris a few weeks before when he was looking for housing. I was happy for Jason but a little jealous that it seemed so easy for him to get a date. Considering I had not even come out of the closet at this point, a date seemed out of the question, but I was hoping that some day I would be lucky enough to go on a same-sex date. I was out of D.C. and living in a city that was dripping with decadence where everyone had the savior faire of an aristocrat. I thought that I totally fit in; that is, until I returned to my college dorm room that night. How could I fit in with all of my glamorous new friends if I was stuck in my tiny college dorm room with my crazy drug-dealing roommate? I figured I would just ride it out until senior year of college, when I would graduate and become an amazing Broadway superstar. Even though I could not sing, dance or act, I determined a career in the theatre was just what my future held.

After a few short weeks, Jason and I quickly became the hottest things to hit the West Village piano bar circuit since the sheet music for *Hair* became available to the public. Men our fathers age, or older, would buy us drinks by the dozens and Jason and I sang our hearts out for anyone who would listen. It was a fabulous way to usher in our new lifestyle. However, after weeks of singing show-tunes in piano bars in the West Village with men over twice my age, I had still not come out of the closet, as if at this point, I really needed to.

One night, after a few cocktails, Jason approached me:

"Are you gay now?" he asked.

"Soon," I replied.

"Well, my friend Greg from school thinks you are cute," he whispered in my ear, "go over and talk to him."

From across the room, I began to size Greg up. He was pretty cute from what I could tell. He had red hair and a dorky smile and was just about perfect for what I was looking for. Before I had even come out of the closet, I already had a type: dorks. I love dorks so much. They are so cute with their little glasses and stubby little hands and are usually freaks in bed. They also really come in handy if you need tech support for just about anything. I looked at Greg from across the bar and gave him a smile. He winked back at me and I walked over to talk to him.

"Hey," I said as I put out my hand to shake his, "I'm Mark."

"Like Mark from *Rent*?" he replied.

This was already the gayest conversation I had ever had up until this point and he had only said four words to me, but we were in a piano bar, so what was I to expect?

"Yes," I replied, "like Mark from *Rent*."

"I loved *Rent*," he said. We looked at each other with blank faces for about twelve seconds. Was this as far as our conversation was going to go?

"Oh," he then replied, "I'm Greg"

"Well, it's nice to meet you, Greg."

"Where are you from?" he asked

"D.C." I said nervously. "Well...actually, I am from Maryland, like right outside of D.C., but, I think it's easier to tell people that I am from D.C. because no one has ever heard of where I am really from. It's just like two minutes outside of D.C., totally not far, but no one has ever heard of it." Had I gone completely retarded? I was so nervous about my first potential gay hook-up that I was standing there giving him a verbal tour of the D.C. Metropolitan Area. "Where are you from?"

"Michigan, a small town no one has ever heard of," Greg replied.

"Oh," I said as I stood there and stared at the floor. I had no idea what gay guys spoke about upon first meeting, so we just kind of stared at each other. Across the room, a big forty-year old hairy queen was belting out "Some People" and Greg and I shifted our attention to him.

As the queen was reaching the bridge, Greg looked over at me and smiled. He was adorable. If I were to hook up with him tonight, I could get some action from a guy and have him fix my computer in the morning. It was win-win.

"But, not ROOOOOSSSSSEEEEE!" the queen belted. Everyone cheered as the gayest man on earth finished singing one of the gayest songs on earth. After the clapping subsided, Greg turned to me:

"I was Tulsa in the Kalamazoo production of *Gypsy* a few years back."

"Nice," I replied, "I was the Mayor in the Bethesda, Maryland production of *The Music Man*."

Then, nothing. Conversation stopped again. Greg and I were both fresh out of the closet and neither one of us knew the proper etiquette of the hook-up. Apparently, listing off all of the community theatre productions we had done in high school would suffice for now. A few weeks later, I would come to realize that there is no need for words at all when trying to get a guy to hook-up with you. Now, things were virginal and needed to be taken slowly.

"So…" I said, "where do you live?"

"Upper East Side," Greg replied.

"Nice," I replied.

"Do you want to come check out my place?"

I was not really interested in his place but was interested in him so I agreed to check out his place. I later learned that "check my place out" is gay code for "let's get it on." As I was leaving the bar with Greg, Jason pulled me aside.

"I knew it!" Jason said.

"What?" I asked.

"I knew you were gay."

"Jesus Christ Jason," I replied, "I went to a summer camp for the performing arts where everyone called me Natalie because they thought I looked like Natalie from *The Facts of Life*, and I allowed them to do it. All the while performing in a production of *Sugarbabies* in nursing homes all across the Catskills. If that isn't a fucking fag, then I don't know what is. It doesn't take a fucking genius to call a spade a spade." Baby's first gay tangent. I was making progress. Jason smiled as Greg and I left the bar, headed for the elusive Upper East Side.

Greg and I got into a cab and went up to his place on the Upper East Side. Once inside, we made the usual small talk:

"I remember when I was doing *Bye, Bye Birdie* at a dinner theatre in Rockville," I said as Greg poured me a glass of Royal Vodka into a paper cup. "I got so nervous when I was on stage doing hurkies, I ended up falling on my ass!"

"That's hilarious!" Greg said as he handed me an alcohol filled paper cup. "I once peed myself when I was doing a production of *The Sound of Music* as a child. It was super embarrassing, but I was only six."

We both laughed. I don't know if we were laughing at the fact that we had both humiliated ourselves in front of hundreds of people or that we were having the most ridiculous conversation two men had ever had but we laughed nonetheless. As the laughing subsided, Greg leaned in and kissed me thus beginning the most awkward hook-up that has ever taken place. Two eighteen year old guys who had never hooked up with someone of the same sex before attempting to be sexy. The result: something that would have been a classic episode of *America's Funniest Home Videos*.

"I really like him," I said into the phone the next day.

Jason, who was relieved I had finally done something about my homosexuality proclaimed: "I am so happy that you *finally* came out of the closet. I knew it was only a matter of time, but damn did that take forever."

"I think he may be the one," I said.

"Mark, you hardly know him. You just hooked up, see how it goes."

"I don't know Jason, I am pretty interested in him," I replied. I was acting like a straight up lesbian. I already had plans of moving in with him and raising his children.

"Just see where it goes, Mark. Don't rush anything. You are just coming out of the closet," Jason said. Then suddenly, the topic changed back to drinking, "hey, I know, why don't we go out tonight? My father just gave me money for books, we can use it to get wasted tonight." Jason decided my coming out was a good reason for us to get hammered together. Soon it would become tradition that everything from a good grade to a hangnail was reason to get hammered together.

"I can't, I have to study. I have exams coming up," I replied. School was definitely getting in the way of my social activities, but that was what I was in New York to do in the first place so I had to put forth some effort.

"Fine," Jason said, defeated. "Call me this weekend, and we'll go out." I hung up with Jason and got to work.

A few days later, I was beginning to worry because I had not heard from Greg. It had been three days and I had not so much as heard a peep from him on instant messenger and began wondering what was going on. Finally, after five days of not hearing from him, I gave him a call, but it went straight to voicemail.

"Hey Greg, it's Mark from the other night," I said into his voicemail box. "You know, like Mark from *Rent*, ha, ha, ha." What the hell is wrong with me? "Just calling to see if you wanted to get together sometime soon. Maybe we could catch a show or something. I would love to see *Chicago* or even *Annie Get Your Gun*. You know, that was the first show I was ever in and now Bernadette Peters is doing it on Broadway. I love the story of Annie Oakley." I would continue with the rest of the message I left him, but I am afraid it gets a little too embarrassing even for me. I had no idea what I was doing so I continued rambling on until his voicemail cut me off. I could not remember whether or not I told him to call me, so I called him back and left another message reminding him to call me back. After a few days of not hearing from him, I began to worry so I called Jason and the two of us met at our favorite piano bar.

"I don't get it," I said as I sipped my Manhattan. I had upgraded from Whiskey Sours to Manhattans in a matter of weeks. "Why hasn't he called me back?"

Jason looked at me as if I was a child who was just told the Easter Bunny wasn't real. "Mark, honey," he said, cocktail in hand, "I've been doing this a while and I have to let you in on a secret. What you did last weekend was a meaningless hook-up. Greg is not going to call you back because he was not interested in anything more than a hook-up. That's how we gays do things."

"Wait…what?" I replied.

"Mark, it was a hook-up. Get over it!"

Jason and I drank our cares away. We drank Goldschlager and White Russians for the rest of the night and I got sick off of alcohol for the first time. After getting loaded that night, I woke up the next day vowing to get over Greg and move on. He was my first hook-up after all and I felt it was going to take some time to get over. However, Greg had left me with a little present that was going to forever ingrain him in my memory.

"You have scabies," Dr. Huxtable said to me the next day. My doctor in New York barred a striking resemblance to Bill Cosby and every time he walked in the room I thought he was going to do a stupid dance or offer me Jell-O.

"What the hell is scabies?" I asked as I itched every inch of my body.

"It's like body lice," Dr. Huxtable said with a smile, although I did not find his response charming or funny. "I will give you a cream that will get rid of it. You have to go home and wash everything. Every towel, every sheet, every article of clothing must be washed. Clean everything and use the cream I give you and it will go away in no time."

I shrugged. Of course the first time I hook-up with a guy I get an STD. Just my luck.

"Just use the cream to make key lime pie," Dr. Huxtable then said.

"What?" I asked quizzically.

"Just use the cream and you'll be fine," he said.

"Oh."

I sat and stared at the doctor wondering what Phylicia Rashad was doing with her career. How had I come to this? That afternoon, I called Greg and told him to go fuck himself for giving me scabies and to lose my number, which he apparently already had done as I had not heard from him in two weeks now. And so, the Great Scabies Debacle of 2000 kicked into high gear.

I went home and washed everything in my dorm room. As I was doing this, my straight pot-dealing roommate looked on. Probably because he was high. I washed everything and used the cream and felt relieved. However, the next morning, when I woke up, I saw that my roommate was itching all over.

"What the hell is wrong with me?" my roommate asked.

"What's up?"

"I am itchy all over."

Oh shit, I thought. I had somehow given him scabies. Then I remembered when we first moved into our dorm room, I commented on the fact that we both had the exact same towels and we had better be careful not to mix them up. Apparently, someone had and now my roommate had scabies as well. But, it didn't end there. He had given it to his girlfriend, and she had given it to her roommate Meegan (pronounced Meegan. Not Megan. Upon meeting her, I told her that I thought her name was ridiculous and that I would be referring to her simply as Megan or Sara. I thought she looked more like a Sara anyway). For a week, the four of us sat around my dorm room, scratching ourselves like monkeys in a cage. Everyone wondered where the mysterious scabies outbreak originated, but I kept mum. I did not need everyone knowing I had slept with a dirty boy on the Upper East Side.

After the scabies outbreak calmed down, my best friend from high school, Evelyn came up to New York to visit. It was time for me to come out of the closet to her. I always suspected that Evelyn knew I was gay and was just waiting for me to come out, but nothing prepared me for her response to me coming out of the closet.

"So, I got us tickets to go see *Chicago*," I said as Evelyn and I were walking down Broadway with the lights of Times Square upon us, "oh, and I'm gay now."

Evelyn stopped dead in her tracks.

"What?" she asked.

"I'm gay now."

"Gay?"

Apparently Evelyn had forgotten how to speak English in the two months we had been away from each other.

"How are *you* gay?" she asked.

Had she forgotten the night that we drove around D.C. singing every single lyric to the entire CD of ABBA Gold?

"I'm gay, Evelyn," I said. "We all knew it was only a matter of time before I came out of the closet." Evelyn's face went lax. I could see she was extremely disappointed by this dramatic revelation. "Seriously Evelyn, the signs were always there. For God's sake, for our tenth grade English project on *Othello* I wrote a script for a play and based it off of the characters on *All My Children*. How is that *not* the gayest thing anyone has ever done?"

"I know Mark, but I thought," Evelyn paused. "I thought you would always be my back-up guy."

"Come again?"

"My back up guy," she said again, "you know, if I couldn't find a husband by the time I was thirty, you would be there for me."

"Well, let me just put my life on the backburner and wait twelve years to see if you do or do not get married."

"Oh, Mark, you know what I mean."

After about an hour of explaining to Evelyn that I not only liked musical theatre, Britney Spears, soap operas and ABBA, but also dick, she finally got the message. Since then Evelyn has become the perfect fag-hag. Accompanying me to weddings, galas and pretty much any family event I needed her to go to with me. Coming out to Evelyn was an easy segue into coming out to my parents, which was made even easier by my sister who decided to come out the same night. That was a memorable Thanksgiving for everyone in the Rosenberg clan.

Freshman year of college was a really enlightening experience. Not only was I exploring the many possibilities of what academia had to offer (i.e. beer funnels, beer pong, etc.), I was also on a personal mission to try just about anything anyone put in front of me. I had gotten over my fear of hooking up with a guy, and although I contracted an STD, I was no longer afraid. After that, I tried every type of booze imaginable and then moved on to bigger and better things. November of my freshman year of college, I had the pleasure of meeting my new BFF, Alex who would become a staple in my life for the next year or so. Alex and I were very much alike. He lived on the sixteenth floor of my dorm building and the two of us quickly bonded over our mutual love of Ace of Base. We became fast friends and began hanging out almost every evening. We had even found a new hang out, Club Blue.

One night after we had been pre-gaming in Alex's dorm room we headed down to Club Blue with full intentions of getting blackout drunk. Upon entering we did the usual shooters and began flirting with guys for free drinks. We were eighteen and poor college students, so we had to work with what we had. I ended up befriending a really hot guy, whose name I do not remember, so I will refer to him as "the hot guy." We were flirting pretty hardcore until he pulled me aside and took me to the bathroom.

As we entered the bathroom, he emptied his pockets and pulled out a small plastic baggie and a rolled up twenty dollar bill.

"What are you doing?" I asked the hot guy.

"Coke," he replied.

"Oh," I said as I watched him put the twenty-dollar bill into his left nostril and snort up the cocaine he had laid out on the toilet paper holder. Suddenly, the allure of doing coke was lost on me. It wasn't nearly as glamorous as when they did it in *Boogie Nights* and Julianne Moore flipped out on Roller Girl and told her she would be her mother.

"Want some?" the hot guy asked as he whipped his nose.

"Ummm…ok," I replied. And why not? What is the worst that could happen? "Can you just give me just a second?" I asked. The hot guy left me alone in the bathroom to contemplate whether or not to do the drugs that sat before me. I really wanted to look cool in front of the hot guy, but was nervous about doing coke. I then wondered what life would be like if I started doing drugs. Was I to end up like a junkie or someone fabulous like Liza Minnelli who was pretty much coked up throughout the 70's? As I pondered what do, an apparition appeared in the bathroom.

"Say no to drugs," the figure said.

I could not see who was standing before me. I had so much to drink that I was not sure if I was hallucinating or seeing a real person. As the figure came closer, I knew exactly who it was.

"Say no to drugs!" the figure said again.

I wiped my eyes and saw a little old lady in a red pantsuit approaching me.

"Damn you Nancy Reagan!" I yelled. She had come to me again. Nancy first came to me in a vision when I smoked weed for the first time, and now she was back.

"I warned you that pot was the gateway drug, and look at you," Nancy said as she gestured toward the pile of cocaine that was sitting on the toilet paper holder. "Now you are about to take cocaine. Shame on you Mark."

"But Nancy, I really want to hook up with that hot guy," I said. Surely Nancy Reagan understood the ins and outs of gay life in New York. She was kind of like a fag-hag with all of those power suits.

"Oh, you homosexuals and your drugs," she said with a laugh. "I have come to so many of you and no one ever listens. Look at what happened to Paul Lynde for Christ's sake!"

"Maybe you are right Nancy," I said. Then suddenly, I remembered why I had not listened to Nancy Reagan in the first place. "Wait a minute, Nance. I remember why I didn't listen to you before. You stole Ronald Reagan away from my beloved Jane Wyman, star of *Falcon Crest*, the best show ever on television. I'm not listening to a word you say. Don't tell me not to drugs after you went around stealing another woman's man!" And with that I took the rolled up twenty dollar bill and snorted the cocaine.

"Remember my dear, crack is wack," Nancy said.

"Whatever," I replied, "your husband's administration was a joke!" And with that Nancy disappeared.

While this very special episode of *Diff'rent Stokes* was taking place in the club bathroom, the hot guy was outside knocking on the door.

"You OK in there?" the hot guy asked.

I opened the door and replied:

"Yeah, I am fine. Just hashing out a few things with Nancy Reagan."

He looked dumbfounded. "Pretty good shit, huh?" he asked.

Good shit indeed. We partied the night away. Cocaine was fabulous for me because while taking it, I could drink as much alcohol as I wanted without getting drunk or sick. It was like a miracle drug and I wondered why more people didn't do it. That is until the next morning. I awoke the next morning wondering what I had done wrong to deserve feeling the way I felt. I felt as if someone had dropped a ton of bricks on my head and left me for dead. My head was spinning and I felt as if I my heart was going to stop at any moment. I told myself that I was never going to drink or do drugs ever again, but that night rolled around and it was time to party again. Alex and I had cleverly decided that from then on we were going to have themed nights of going out. Every night of the week we would dress up in a different theme. It seemed to be the perfect way to try and find a new boyfriend. Heroin chic was a favorite, where we would temporarily dye our hair black, put black eyeliner on and tight jeans and look like crack heads. For whatever reason, we thought this look was attractive; but, after a while, I realized we didn't even need the makeup anymore. We were pretty much crack heads.

One night before Christmas during freshman year of college, Alex and I decided that it would be fun to try acid. I had done mushrooms in high school and was told that the effects were similar but acid was even more potent. The two of us went to a club and danced and drank and had a gay old time. After a few hours of dancing, Alex put a tab of acid onto my tongue and I immediately cased the club for Nancy Reagan. I couldn't find her, but I did see a drag queen in a red pillbox hat that bared a striking resemblance to her. I guess Nancy had given up on me – I was a lost cause now. I had reached the point of no return, although I did tell myself I would never smoke crack or shoot up heroin. At least I still had some boundaries.

The night we tripped on acid was like taking a trip on an emotional rollercoaster on which I care to never ride again. A club promoter named Stephan came up to me and tried to kiss me and his face turned into a bat then he tried to swallow me whole. Then, the walls began to melt and I tried to lick them because I thought they had turned into milkshakes. Finally, I was so hungry when I got home that I made myself some macaroni and cheese that turned into worms and I hid under my bed for a solid hour until I thought it was safe to come out.

The next day, I met up with Jason for a few drinks at our piano bar.

"Where the hell have you been?" Jason asked.

"Having visions of Nancy Reagan and trying every drug imaginable," I replied.

"What?" he asked.

"Never mind," I said. All of the experimentation had taken its toll on me. "I don't feel well."

"Drink this," Jason said as he waved a martini in my face. "Vodka is good for the heart."

"I can't do drugs anymore. It's only been a month and I feel like a junkie already," I said. My Jewish guilt wouldn't even allow me to be a drug addict without feeling horrible about it.

"Just take a break," Jason said. "Just drink. Drinking is fun and it won't kill you."

Why do I always think everything everyone tells me is the truth?

"You're right!" I proclaimed, "drinking won't kill me, will it?" Just ruin every relationship I ever had from that point on and force me into making the worst decisions any human could possibly make.

"Cheers to you, Mark," Jason said. "You've overcome your drug addiction." We clinked glasses and both sipped our martinis.

"Wow, it's so easy to get yourself off of drugs. It's a wonder why more people can't do it," I said as I was probably still tripping on the acid from the night before.

"Well, never say never Mark. You know marijuana is a drug."

"Really?"

"So is cocaine."

"Let's just say I won't do any drugs that don't come from mother earth. Since you have to grow weed and cocoa plants, I think that is a safer bet, don't you?" I asked.

"It's a lot healthier for you. God only knows what people put in those acid tabs."

Thus my philosophy on life began and spanned throughout the next decade. My first few months in New York had not only taught me that it was OK to be gay, but also OK to financially support every drug dealer and bartender in the New York metropolitan area for the next eight years.

THE PICK-UP ARTIST

When you're single and living in the big city, there is nothing better than long nights out with your friends, searching for your next lover. We have found, as a culture, that drinking and socializing at bars has been a foolproof way of getting someone into the sack. There is something about alcohol that lowers inhibitions and makes people more willing to do things or sleep with people that they normally wouldn't. For me, going out and drinking let me create a world in which, only I exist. I am not above creating fake professions, wild nonsensical back-stories, or faux celebrity relatives to get someone to notice me. I completely lose my bullshit filter and it's anyone's guess what ridiculous nonsense would come flying out of my mouth. The following are a few situations that I have gotten myself into that have proved disastrous in finding that new lover.

* * * * * * * * * * * *

After moving to New York, my friend Valerie gave me her friend Ashley's brother's fake ID. Tired of missing out on the fun of going out with everyone else, I accepted it, but there were some clear discrepancies between the ID and me. For one, it said my name was Brennan Kasperzack. My name is Mark Rosenberg, however my middle name happens to be Brennan, so it seemed meant to be. Secondly, it said I was six feet, two inches tall. I stand at a mighty five feet, eight inches tall. Brennan has dark brown hair and I have blonde hair. Brennan has brown eyes and mine are blue. There were so many clear differences between my ID and I that I never thought in a million years it would work, but time and time again, it never failed to get me where I needed to be.

After about a year of using it, I got pretty cocky. It didn't seem to matter that I was not who I claimed to be so I continued the charade. One night, when a group of friends and I were out at our favorite bar, Posh, the bouncer came over to me.

"Hey," he said. You have to appreciate the rituals of the gay male mating call.

"What's going on?" I asked.

"Nothing much, just thought I would come over and say 'hi'. I have seen you in here a lot lately."

"Yea, my friends and I love this place. The drinks are strong and the dancing is always so much fun."

"You're name is Brennan, right?" he asked.

"What?" I said with confusion.

"Brennan. You're name is Brennan, right? I remember it from your ID."

"Ummm…yes, of course it is. My name is Brennan. Brennan Kasperzack."

"What are your plans for the evening?"

"Not much. Just hanging out here."

We were at a loss for conversation. After about ten drinks, the only conversation I am usually up for is one that revolves around ABC soaps or a dance off. Sensing he wasn't a fan of *One Life to Live*, I dragged him onto the dance floor and we began dancing.

"You're from Ohio, right?" he yelled over the music as we were dancing.

"What?" I yelled back.

"You're from Ohio, right?" I had forgotten that my alter ego Brennan Kasperzack was from Columbus, Ohio.

"Yea." I yelled back.

"Me too," he said. Fuck. I had never been to Ohio and was too drunk to lie about anything so I just continued dancing. "Columbus, right?"

"Uh, yes," I said. "Brennan Kasperzack from Columbus, Ohio."

"I am from Columbus," he said.

Great. I tried to pull away from him on the dance floor. There was simply no way I could continue to have a conversation about a place I had never been to, let alone lived in.

He followed me as I sat down on a barstool.

"I think you are really cute," he said. "I thought you were really cute the first time I saw you come in here."

"Thanks," I said. "You're really hot." All tact had seemed to fly out the door.

"Where in Columbus did you grow up?" he asked.

Were we really still talking about Ohio? Surely there must have been something more interesting we could have spoken about. Having remembered my fake address, I replied:

"15409 Cherry Vale Road," I replied.

"Oh my God, I lived down the street on Rolling Bluff Road."

Seriously? How the hell was it possible that this guy lived down the street from the real Brennan Kasperzack?

"What a coincidence."

"What high school did you go to?" he asked.

"Private school," I replied. I figured that was a good way to get out of making something even more ridiculous up.

"Holy Child?" he asked.

"Sure," I replied.

"Oh my God, I went there too!" he said. "What year did you graduate?"

"2000," I said, hoping he wasn't going to catch me in a lie.

"No wonder you look familiar. I graduated in 1998. We must have crossed paths at some point in high school," he said as he was patting my back.

"Wow, what a small world," I said as I signaled the bartender over to refill my drink.

"Want to come back to my place for a nightcap?" he asked.

I did, but I certainly could not continue talking about the goings on in Columbus, Ohio.

"Sure," I responded, "Let's not talk about Ohio anymore. I have really bad memories about that place. My father used to beat me. The first chance that I got I left and I will never go back to Ohio. Columbus, Ohio, where I am from. I really don't even like talking about my past."

"That's horrible," as he said this Valerie and the rest of my party were approaching. I gave her a *leave-me-alone* look, but she came up anyway.

"Mark, where the hell have you been?" she asked in my direction. I pretended to ignore her. I was Brennan Kasperzack now and Brennan Kasperzack was going to hook up with the hot bouncer. "Mark!" Valerie yelled in my ear, "we are leaving, now. Let's go."

"Who's Mark?" the bouncer asked.

"I have no idea who this girl is," I said referring to my good friend Valerie.

"Mark, let's go," Valerie said once more.

"Who is Mark?" the bouncer asked.

"Mark," Valerie said as she gestured toward me. "Mark Rosenberg."

"You? You're Jewish?" he said as he looked me deep in the eyes.

"I have no idea who this girl is," I continued, "my name is Brennan Kasperzack from Columbus, Ohio. Are you lost little girl?"

"Fuck you," Valerie said, "Let's go."

"I am sorry miss, but I think you have the wrong person. His name isn't Mark, it's Brennan." It was as if Valerie had completely blacked out and forgotten it was she who had given me the fake ID in the first place.

"His name is Mark," she replied, "I've known this homo for seven years. We grew up together in D.C."

"I thought you said you were from Columbus," the bouncer said.

I didn't know what to do. If the bouncer found out that I was lying, I would not only not get laid, but never be allowed into Posh again. I had to think quickly. I looked at Valerie, looked at the bouncer and turned away. I then ran out the door, never to return to Posh again until after my 21st birthday.

* * * * * * * * * * * * *

The evening before I was supposed to go home for Christmas break, sophomore year of college, my friend Jason and I decided to celebrate the fact that we had made it out of another semester of college alive. We decided to head down to The Park, which was a really trendy bar at the time in the west twenties that hosted an all-gay event every Sunday evening. Jason and I agreed, on the way down, to a three-martini limit because we both had to catch an 8:30 train the next morning. One thing led to another, as it usually does, and before we knew it, it was two in the morning and both Jason and I were severely trashed. It had been a really difficult semester and I felt a long girls' night out was long overdue and well deserved. As Jason and I continued drinking, I spotted a really hot model-type standing at the opposite end of the bar. I gave him a drunk half wink and walked over. Before, walking over, Jason grabbed me.

"Oh my God, Mark," Jason yelled into my ear, "it's Boy George!" Across the room stood Boy George, and his entourage of British teenaged hangers on. Jason had had a man crush on Boy George since he had been able to apply his own lip-liner, so this was quite the sighting for him.

"Go talk to him," I said. I was trying to get Jason out of my way so I could talk to the hot model at the end of the bar. Jason was notorious for accidental drunken cock blocks, so I needed to get him out of my way in order to make my move. Jason walked over to Boy George and I approached my model.

"Hi," I said to the Adonis that stood before me.

"What's up?" he said.

"Nothing," I said as I put my hand out to shake his, "my name is Mark."

"Jared," he replied.

We made the usual small talk, but I could tell he was not interested. I had to think of something quick to draw his attention back to me.

"So what do you do for a living?" I asked.

"I'm a model, but I am trying to get into acting." Of course he was.

"That's amazing. I was a teen model for Dockers in the JC Penny catalogue." There goes my drunken word vomit. When I drink, it's like I get full of Tourettes and shit just comes flying out of my mouth.

"Cool," he replied, "what do you do for a living now?"

I had to think quickly. Being a student and waiting tables is not nearly as glamorous as something I could lie about. Besides, he would never find out if I made something up. "I'm a casting director for *All My Children*," I said.

"Really?" he asked.

"Yes," I had my awkward half smile on, as if I had just had a stroke. I always get a half-lazy face when I am drunk and lying.

"I have an audition for *All My Children* right after New Year's." Of course he did. Now being borderline obsessed with Susan Lucci does not a casting director make. I had absolutely no idea how to follow that remark so I just replied:

"Oh, let me give you my card so you can call me before the audition," I said. Apparently, I had fake cards to go along with my fake job. "We can go over lines together. I am just warning you now, that you will most likely have to take your shirt off." I searched my pockets for my "card" and told him that I must have left them in my other pants. I gave him my number and told him to call me.

All and all it was a great night out. A hot model had gotten my number and a D-list celebrity from the 80's had manhandled Jason. I passed out that night and woke up the next day at four in the afternoon having missed my train home for the holidays.

I had completely forgotten that I even met anyone that night until a few weeks later when I got a message from Jared: "Hey Mark, it's Jared from The Park. Just wondering if I could come over to your place and run over lines with you. My audition is in a few days and I would love some pointers. Give me a call."

My fake profession had caught up with me. Previously when I had told people that I was Angelina Jolie's stunt double or Ray Charles's Seeing Eye dog, people knew I was lying immediately and didn't bother. This guy was totally buying it. Models are usually not the brightest crayons in the box, but I figured if he came over to my college dorm room to run lines, he would have had enough sense to know I was lying. I had to think quickly. I picked up the phone and called him back, but it went straight to voicemail. I left a message:

"Hey Jared, it's Mark. Sorry I missed you, but it's been chaos on the set. We just found out that the girl who plays Maggie is pregnant so we are either going to need to recast or rework a whole six months worth of storyline. I have a feeling that she may just get raped and become pregnant with her rapist's baby and be torn about what to do, but you never know with these things. Anyway, good luck with the audition and give me a call if you need anything."

How layered and elaborate. There was no way he would ever find out that I was completely bullshitting him.

I never ended up hearing from Jared again. Probably because once he got there, he realized that I had absolutely nothing to do with *All My Children* and that the girl who played Maggie was totally not preggers. Next time I create a faux profession for myself, I am going to have to do a little more research beforehand.

* * * * * * * * * * * * *

I had met a few friends out at Therapy one night for a few psychotic episodes. Therapy is a bar in Hell's Kitchen that serves the most delicious drinks in New York called psychotic episodes. For a while, they were my favorite drink. It's basically just a bunch of liquor dumped into a glass but it tastes like fruit punch. I had tried to master the recipe at home, but never could so I began to frequent Therapy so I could get my lips around the delicious cocktail. The thing about psychotic episodes is that they go down really easily and before you know it, you are drunk off your ass. I had about six of them on the night in question and went outside to get some air and smoke a few cigarettes. When I got outside, there was a handsome man smoking, so I struck up a conversation.

"I'm Mark," I said.

"Eric," he replied as we shook hands. He was hot and he smoked so things were looking good already.

"Are you here by yourself?" I asked.

"My friends just left. I am procrastinating going home. I have to move in the morning."

"That sucks. I hate moving." Having done it about seven times in three years, it was not something I ever wanted to do again.

"Yea, me too," he replied. "I am so not ready. I'm packed, but I have no idea how I am going to move. I have not hired movers yet."

"I'll help you." There goes my drunken Tourettes again. Not only did I hate moving myself, I hated helping other people move even more. I guess it must have been the six cocktails talking but at the time, it sounded like a really great idea.

"Really?" his eyes lit up.

Fuck. Did this guy think I was serious? I was really just trying to get laid. I would be in no condition to move my neck in the morning, let alone his bookshelf.

"Sure, why not?" I replied.

I ditched my friends and got into a cab with Eric. We chatted on the ride up but I don't really remember what we were talking about. The drinks were strong and sweet and I was beginning to feel them. Once we got back to Eric's apartment, I noticed there were boxes packed and a few things scattered about. We sat down on his couch and began making out. A few moments later, Eric pulled out a bottle of scotch and poured two glasses. I had sworn off brown liquor years before after a mishap involving a bottle of Jim Beam and a few lesbians, which I care never to discuss again, but I was just drunk enough to accept a drink. We drank and continued making out. The room began to spin so I excused myself to the bathroom. I had way too much to drink and now I was beginning to feel sick.

The next thing I knew, I was sleeping on the bathroom floor under a bathmat, which I had been using as a blanket. The sun was coming in from the bathroom window and hitting my forehead. I got myself up and splashed some water on my face. I guess I drank more than I thought, as my head was ringing. I got myself together and opened the bathroom door. When I peered out of the door, everything in the apartment was missing. The boxes, the television, the couch I had been making out on hours earlier, were all gone. Eric had moved out while I was passed out on the bathroom floor. I looked at the clock on my phone and noticed it was three o'clock in the afternoon. What a gentleman not to wake me up from my twelve-hour slumber on the bathroom floor. Or, had I fallen into a small coma and he tried to wake me, but couldn't? At least I got out of helping a stranger move. I walked out of the vacant apartment and went home. That was the final time I ever offered to help anyone move, drunk or sober.

* * * * * * * * * * * * *

A few months later, Jason and I went down to D.C. for Thanksgiving. I decided to join Jason and his parents for dinner one night that weekend. We went to a bistro that was right next door to a gay club. Jason's dad is nearly deaf and you literally have to scream for him to hear anything. "Colonoscopy, Dad!" Jason yelled at the dinner table after his father asked how my father was doing, "Mark's dad just had a colonoscopy!!!"

"Oh," Jason's dad replied.

Of course, this is inappropriate dinnertime conversation, but with

Jason's family, this is the norm and it is also typical for everyone around you to hear what is going on. It makes for quite an embarrassing evening, so Jason and I decided we would dance it out at the club down the street. On our way over, Jason pulled me aside:

"My mother told me in the bathroom that my Dad is not only going deaf, but blind as well."

"You and your mother go to the bathroom together?" I asked.

"Shut up. On our way to the bathroom…." Jason continued, "whatever, anyway, I don't think she is really happy about the fact that she is going to be living with Helen Keller."

"Yikes," I replied.

"I know," Jason said, "and he is still driving, it's such a mess."

"Well, let's forget about all that and have fun," I said as we entered the club. I always have such pearls of wisdom after a few cocktails.

Jason and I entered the club and tried to have fun. Coming from New York back to D.C. you realize how superior everything in New York is. However, Jason and I manage to have fun wherever we go, with a little help from our friends, Jack, Jim, Jose and Johnny. We drank a ton and as we were dancing, I spotted a group of really cute guys in the corner, talking and moving their hands about. I assumed that they were just really passionate about what they were saying, but Jason informed me that they were deaf.

"That's sign language, you moron!" Jason yelled. Having learned sign language to accommodate his father's dwindling hearing, Jason walked over and began signing something to the boys and they laughed. There he goes again cock blocking me. I walked over to join them and introduced myself, and noticed one of the deaf boys was very attractive.

"Jason, that one is really cute," I said about the boy I was eying.

"Ok, Mark," Jason said. "How on earth are you going to have a conversation with him?"

"Oh, Jason how little you know. In middle school chorus, I had to sign "The Star Spangled Banner" and "I Swear" by All-4-One when we performed at a nursing home. I can wing it." Although, at that point in the evening, the only sign language I remembered was "stars", "moon" and "sky". I could totally make a conversation out of that. Perhaps he was into astrology.

"How do sign 'thank you'?"

I looked at Jason, gave him the finger and walked away. After a few drinks my English usually isn't that great anyway so what difference did it make if he could hear me or not?

I walked over to the cute deaf kid and waved 'hi'. He waved back. I could do this after all. He began signing something and I pretended to understand what he was signing. He signed something else and I decided that having a conversation was not necessary and I dragged him onto the dance floor and tried making out with him. We began dancing and he continued to sign something.

"I DON'T REALLY KNOW SIGN LANGUAGE THAT GREAT!" I yelled into his ear. After remembering he was deaf, I gave him a *I don't know* look and we continued dancing, but I could tell that the deaf kid was drifting away. He kept signing something, but I didn't know what it was so I just kept grabbing him and dancing. I saw Jason yelling something from the other side of the room, but I just ignored him. He was always trying to ruin my fun, but I was not going to let him do it this time. The deaf guy kept on signing and I had no idea what was going on. Finally, Jason intervened.

"Mark, what the hell are you doing?" he asked as he pulled the deaf kid away from me.

"Dancing," I replied. I turned around and the deaf kid disappeared. "Damn it Jason! Thanks for ruining everything!"

"I think you are completely retarded," Jason said. "So much for you 'winging it', you moron."

"What do you mean?"

"The whole time you were dancing with him, he was telling you that he had a boyfriend. The guy he was sitting next to when you walked over to him was his boyfriend."

"Damn All-4-One and their pointless lyrics! It's no wonder their careers were short-lived."

As Jason and I continued talking, a six-foot tall black guy, who was built like a brick shit-house walked over to us. It was the deaf kid's boyfriend.

"Which one of you were trying to steal my man?" the huge man asked two scrawny gay boys. Jason and I looked at each other and ran out the door. Once outside, Jason smacked me upside the head and called me an asshole.

* * * * * * * * * * * * *

A few years later, Jason and I moved into together. We found an apartment on the Upper Upper East Side. Actually, it was more like Spanish Harlem. We decided to coin the name "SpaHa" to make it seem as it we were living somewhere cool.

"Wow Jason, we live on the 6, just like J. Lo.! Isn't this exciting?" I said. It was very exciting for both of us to be living in our own apartment after having lived in student housing for two years. It was cheap and just what we needed. Although it was right next door to a slaughterhouse where they killed chickens and the sound of chickens meeting their maker was rather unappetizing so we opted to eat out every night. Jason and I moved into the new apartment and the shenanigans immediately began. We would host after hours parties just about every weekend and have about seven to ten of our new best friends that we had just met that night over for drinks. One night, our straight new best friend Bill got sick in our toilet and ended up clogging it up. The next day, Jason and I did not know what to do. We had a clogged toilet and about $17 between the two of us. That $17 was most definitely going to have to be spent on drinks that night, so we decided to leave the toilet as is and figure something out at a later date. That's what you get for having straight people over to your apartment. Over the next few weeks, Jason and I managed to make do without having a toilet. We befriended the Chinese lady who owned the restaurant downstairs and she let us use her bathroom whenever we needed it. If it was an emergency, Jason and I both knew what drastic measures to take. That's where the big plastic bags from Key Food came in handy. In actuality, we were the exact opposite of J. Lo.

Jason and I loved living together. Every weekend was a new journey into the unknown. If there was a new gay bar or club, Jason and I would hit it up and we were having the time of our lives. Only one thing lingered, our toilet. I am not exactly sure why it took us so long to have it fixed, but we were young and on the go, and it just didn't seem like a necessity. Booze on the other hand, was totally necessary and consumed in great amounts during the year Jason and I lived together. One night, Jason and I got really hammered at a piano bar that we frequented in the West Village. I had just the right amount of vodka in my system to approach a really hot guy that was eye fucking me from across the room. I stumbled over:

"Hey, Mark," I said. "I mean…wait…my name is Mark."

He laughed: "I'm Michael."

"What's going on?" I asked.

We chatted for a few minutes and it was clear to Michael and I that we would be hooking up that night. Jason saw what was going on from across the room, and in his usual fashion, came over to interrupt.

"Hey guys," Jason said.

"Jason, this is Michael," I said as I introduced him to my latest trick.

Jason and Michael exchanged pleasantries then Jason pulled me aside and whispered in my ear:

"Mark, you can't bring that guy home. Our toilet is broken. If he spends the night, he is going to have to go to the bathroom at some point and he most definitely cannot use our toilet."

"Damn it!" I replied, "maybe I can go to his." Jason walked away and I gave him a *thanks-for-the-reminder* smack on the ass as he walked away. I refocused my attention on Michael.

"So, do you want to get out of here?" I casually asked Michael.

"Yes!" he replied.

"Should we head out to yours?" I asked.

"No, we can't, I live in a studio with another guy and we agreed not to bring people back to our place."

"Oh."

"Why can't we just go back to your place?"

"Well…" I said. I couldn't tell him that our toilet had been clogged for the past two months and that he would have to pee out of the window if he needed to go to the bathroom.

"Is that Jason kid your boyfriend?"

I laughed until I almost chocked and replied: "Of course not. Jason is my best friend. We are just having some problems at our apartment."

"I really want to hook up with you," Michael said. Damn it. Why hadn't we fixed the toilet weeks ago? Why did we suck at life so much that now I was missing a night in bed with a total hottie? I tried to think of an elaborate lie to tell him, but I was too drunk to lie, something that never happened.

"Well, you can come over if you want," I said as Michael's eyes lit up. "But, if you have to go the bathroom you'll have to pee out of the window; and if you need to take a shit, I am afraid that you will have to go in a plastic bag or run down to the Chinese restaurant downstairs. Just tell Ming, that you are with Jason and I, she knows us."

His face went from a smile to a face of utter disgust.

"Are you serious?" he said.

"Yes," I replied. "Our toilet is broken."

"That is the most disgusting request anyone has ever asked of me. You people should be ashamed of the way you live," he said as he grabbed his coat and walked out the door.

The one time I don't lie about my life I don't get laid. Typical.

HOW TO TURN A STRAIGHT MAN GAY IN TWENTY MINUTES OR LESS

Hobbies are fun. For most people, hobbies are something that allow them to get away from everyday responsibilities and do something different. Many people enjoy sports or the arts as a hobby. In college, my hobby was forcing seemingly straight guys to come out of the closet. For some reason every gay straight man who wants to come out of the closet comes to me for guidance. I don't know how I do it, but I have turned straight men gay faster than Bette Midler can sing "The Boogie Woogie Bugle Boy of Company B." The following are some tips in helping that cute 'maybe-gay-guy' find his way out of the closet.

MISSION NUMBER ONE: ZACK

HOMOSEXUAL TENDENSIES: Yoga, General love of theatre and Britney Spears.

Junior year of college, I moved into a hotel. It was the most wonderful option for student housing anyone had ever thought of. It was perfect for me because the usual annoyances of student housing were not present. Gone were the student aides and non-smoking rooms. Living in the hotel allowed me to do pretty much whatever I wanted and the shenanigans ensued. Shortly after moving into the hotel, I met a really cute guy named Zack. He lived on my floor, but went to a different school and the two of us became fast friends. I was always telling him that he needed to come out with me because all of my straight girlfriends from school were really cute and after a few drinks, pretty easy.

That Valentine's Day, my friend Candace, whom I had told Zack about, and I had gone out and gotten completely wasted. So wasted that the two of us were vomiting out of the cab on our way home. Candace was too sick to make it back to her apartment all the way in Brooklyn so she decided to stay with me. I put her drunken ass in bed and was beginning to get ready for bed myself when I heard a knock on the door. I opened it and was surprised to see Zack.

"Hey Zack, what's up?" I asked.

"Nothing, man. Just went out for Valentine's drinks with some friends from school and got pretty wasted," he said.

"Fun," I said. Zack peered in and saw that Candace was passed out on my bed, possibly in a coma.

"Is that your friend you wanted me to meet?" he asked.

"Yea. We had a bit too much to drink. I think she is out for the night," I said.

"Oh well. Why don't you come hang out in the lobby with me before you go to bed?" he asked.

"Sure," I said. Zack left and I finished brushing my teeth and went to the lobby to meet him. He was sitting in a chair smoking a cigarette. "Hey, man," he said, "I fucking hate Valentine's Day"

"Yea. Me too. Candace and I always end up spending it together and always end up getting blackout drunk. It's a shame you couldn't meet her, she really is a nice girl."

"Oh, well maybe next time," Zack said as he got out of the chair he was sitting in and moved to the floor. Once on the floor, he began doing yoga positions that were a bit provocative. I watched this cute boy maneuver around the lobby floor, and since I had so much to drink and my bullshit filter was completely gone I blurted out:

"If you keep moving around like that I am going to have to have sex with you."

Zack stopped and looked at me. "Ok," he said.

"Wait…what? I thought you were straight."

"Not really. I mean, I have never hooked up with a guy before, but I have always wanted to. We're friends, so we might as well just do it."

This was amazing. Nothing is better than Valentine's Day booty, especially from a straight guy. I told him that we obviously could not do it in my room because Candace was asleep in my bed. Although she probably was so drunk that she would not have even noticed that two guys were having homosexual sex next to her, I didn't want to risk it. He told me that his roommate was home and we could not go to his room. He then told me that there was a room on the top floor of the hotel that was filled with old mattresses that no one knew about that we could hook up in. I told him that we needed to get up there immediately. I was getting excited and we needed to move this along.

We went up to the room that was filled with mattresses on the forty-fifth floor of the hotel. It had an amazing view of Central Park and had I been with anyone else, it may have almost been romantic, but Zack and I were both very drunk and I am not sure that Zack really knew what he was getting himself into. We sat down on the pile of mattresses and began making out. After a few seconds, Zack began crying.

"What's wrong?" I asked.

"I can't do this!" he said.

"Can't do what? Make out with me? It was your idea."

"I know," he said sobbing, "but my grandmother is very religious and if she finds out about this, she is going to flip out."

"What?" I said as I looked around, "do you see her here?"

"No."

"Then what the hell are you crying about? No one is going to find out, just relax."

We continued making out until Zack began crying again.

"What is it?" I asked.

"Do you think they bury gay guys in Catholic cemeteries?"

"What?"

"Do you think they bury gay guys in Catholic cemeteries?"

"I don't fucking know, I'm Jewish!" I said. Now I was getting pissed off. All I wanted to do was make out, possibly get a handy j and go to bed and this guy was having a moral dilemma at four in the morning in a room full of mattresses.

"Because if they don't, my parents will find out that I am gay when the Catholic Church refuses to bury me in a Catholic cemetery."

"What?" I was so confused, "are we *really* having this conversation right now?"

"I just don't want to disappoint my family."

"Who is going to fucking find out? We are in a room filled with mattresses that no one knows about but us. Aren't your parents in Arizona? Are you afraid they are going to randomly come in right now?"

"No, but what if you tell someone and it gets back to my parents?" he asked.

"I highly doubt that will happen," I said. I really didn't care that much to be honest. I was horny and drunk and saw an opportunity that I really wanted to jump on, literally.

"I can't do this," he said as he got up.

"Fine," I said.

Zack got up and walked out of the room. I sat on the mattresses and looked out the window to see the amazing view of Central Park after dark. I sat there and thought about the first time I had hooked up with a guy and how awkward it was for me. Perhaps I should have been a bit more understanding with Zack. Perhaps, I should not have downed a pitcher of margaritas earlier, but what was done was done, and I went back to my room and passed out next to Candace, who thankfully was still breathing.

A few months later, I saw Zack in tight jeans and an even tighter shirt en route to the Britney Spears concert at Madison Square Garden. I guess he figured out that gays can be buried in Catholic cemeteries and just went with it.

MISSION NUMBER TWO: DAVID

HOMOSEXUAL TENDENSIES: Likes dick.

A big group of us had met at my friend Stephanie's apartment for a Cinco de Mayo party or Saint Patrick's Day party or something. I don't remember why we were all there, but it was one of those holidays that involved a lot of excessive drinking. Maybe it was Bastille Day, I honestly don't remember, but Stephanie had all of us over including one of her co-worker's high school friends David. David was really cute. He was short and Jewish, just the way I like them. I began chatting with David and ended up flat out asking him if he was a homo. He was well dressed and cute and in New York – all signs pointed gay.

"Of course not," he said as if I was offending him.

"Oh, I just thought…"

"It's OK. A lot of people ask me if I am gay. My parents asked me last weekend," he said with a laugh.

Maybe because you are a big fucking homo, I thought.

We continued chatting and my friend Chad, who was visiting from Atlanta, met up with us. The second Chad walked into the room, David's eye lit up. Now, if David was as straight as he claimed to be, his eyes would have lit up if Halle Berry had walked into the room. But, it wasn't Halle Berry who had walked into the room; it was Chad so my suspicions grew deeper.

"Hey Chad," I said as I waved for him to come over to David and I.

"Hey guys," Chad said.

"Chad, this is my new friend David. David this is Chad." The two shook hands and I could see that David's mouth was almost watering. I smiled knowing tonight was going to be the night that David was coming out of the closet. One of the greatest parts about meeting a stranger and having him come out of the closet right before your very eyes is that you never know when it is going to happen. It's part of the thrill for me. I watched this all go down right in front of me, when I assumed it was going to be a low-key night with the girls. And here we were.

David and Chad chatted for what felt like hours. I stood there and mediated. Meaning, no one was talking to me so I stood there and eavesdropped on their conversation. When David went to refresh his drink, Chad pulled me aside.

"I am going to fuck that little Jewish kid tonight," Chad said, "he is fucking hot!"

"He's straight," I said with air quotes.

"No!" Chad said, "no he isn't. We were just talking about Madonna's last tour. There is no way that kid is straight."

"I am sure he isn't, but he is claiming to be a hetero," I said. All of the sudden, I had a thought and smiled, "Chad, let's get him really drunk and see if he will hook up with you."

I decided I was going to let Chad have this one, but I wanted to be there for the big reveal. We continued drinking the whole night long. When everyone was drunk, Chad suggested that David and I come back to his hotel room with him for a little after party. I knew this was going to be David's coming out party because he was so eager to join us at Chad's.

We all got back to Chad's hotel room, cracked open a bottle of vodka and mixed it with anything we could find. I think it may have been Diet

Coke. We sat around and chatted for a while until I passed out on the bed. A few hours later, I woke up to find Chad and David making out in the bed next to me. Straight my ass.

David and Chad hung out a lot while Chad was in town and after he left, David latched on to me. I questioned David on whether or not he was gay and his response was simple, but greedy:

"I am bisexual," David said.

"Bisexual?" I asked. "Yea, I was bisexual for like a week before I just admitted I was a homo."

"No, I really like girls *and* guys," David said.

"Ok, whatever. Let me know how that works out for you. I don't think a lot of girls find it sexy to find out that the last person you dated may have been named Steve."

David and I continued hanging out and after a couple weeks, David had officially hooked up with all of my gay single friends. Every time I introduced David to a new friend of mine, he would end up hooking up with them. It did not take me too long to realize David was not to be trusted around any of my friends and that my cute little straight boy had turned into an ugly gay monster.

MISSION NUMBER THREE: MICHAEL

HOMOSEXUAL TENDENCIES: Avid love of theatre, distaste of sporting events, took better care of his hair than most girls I know.

Every homo loves gay pride in New York. It's like where homosexuality was born and the events that lead up to pride in New York are like nothing else in the country. For me, it meant a weekend of blackout drinking and hopefully a hook up or two. It's a weekend filled with parties and excess and Pride 2006 was no exception. My friend Roger, who worked at a theatre in Times Square, was hosting a huge party on the theatre's roof and it was to be the party of the year.

I arrived at the party, alone, hoping to find someone to leave with. However, the pickings were very slim. It seemed as though there were mostly lesbians in attendance. I tried to find Roger and ask him what the hell all of these lesbians were doing at his party when someone filled me in that Gay Pride encompassed lesbians as well as gay men. What a disappointment. It didn't matter because shortly after this revelation, I met a little lesbian girl who worked on *Guiding Light* so I started talking to her.

"I fucking hate The *Guiding Light*!" I said. "It's got nothing on my ABC soaps, let me tell you."

"Yes," the lesbian said, "you are right, I have been watching ABC soaps forever, but I got this job and I have to take it. After I started working on *Guiding Light* I starting watching the show and it's really not that bad."

"Whatever dude, they cloned a character," I said. "That's ridiculous!"

"Didn't they go "back in time" on *One Life to Live*?" the lesbian asked.

"Twice," I said. "They went back in time twice, but that's beside the point."

"Ok," she said. As we continued talking, the lesbian's friend came over and introduced himself.

"I'm Michael," he said.

"I'm Mark," I said as I noticed his incredible good looks. His hair was long and shiny and he was perfect. Maybe lesbians aren't useless after all. The lesbian, whose name I cannot remember because, she was a lesbian and I had no use for her, told me that her friend Michael was straight.

"Straight?" I asked after Michael went to the bathroom. "How is he straight? Look at his hair. He takes such good care of it. It's like a Shetland pony – it looks like…manicured. Hair like that takes hours to manage. No straight man has ever had hair like that. There is absolutely no way that guy is straight."

"That's what he claims," the lesbian said, "but I have always had my suspicions."

The lesbian quickly told me about an incident when she was at a party with Michael and he wandered off for hours. When he later resurfaced his perfectly manicured hair was amiss and her other friend Ramon mysteriously went missing.

"Interesting," I said as I sipped my drink. Since it was gay pride and there were literally no gay guys at this event, I thought I needed do some digging. Once Michael came back from the bathroom, I began flirting. Michael was an avid theatre lover and an actor (gay) and so we chatted about the latest theatre gossip.

"*The Drowsy Chaperone* was totally robbed for the Tony!" Michael exclaimed, "*Jersey Boys* was inferior to that masterpiece."

It was quite possibly the gayest conversation I had ever had, but I continued on. As the party began to wind down, I could tell that Michael was a bit tipsy. The lesbian, who was two sheets to the wind, came over and drunkenly told Michael that he should make out with me. Michael swayed back and forth pondering what to do next and before he knew it, I grabbed his shirt collar and stuck my tongue down his throat. We made out in front of everyone at the party but Michael pulled away and laughed it off. I could tell he was totally embarrassed by what had happened and blushed. I excused myself to go the bathroom to freshen up before I left and quickly noticed that I was being followed. Michael was right behind me and followed me in to a stall and we began making out passionately. What is it with gay guys making out in public restrooms? For a group of people that pride themselves on cleanliness they sure do find disgusting places to fornicate. We made out for a while and I invited Michael back to my place. We had sex that night and began an illicit affair that lasted the entire summer. I ended it when Michael decided that he wanted to go back and give girls another try. It didn't work and he is happily an out and proud homosexual prowling the streets of New York City.

You see, all you need is the right amount of alcohol; a dash of curiosity and a hell of a lot of willpower and you too can make that seemingly curious hetero your next sexual conquest.

BOILING POINT

"I am never going to get laid again!" I said as I banged my head against the dinner table. "Never! Never! Never!"

"Chill out, Mark," Tom said. Tom and his boyfriend Michael had just gotten back from a whirlwind summer in Provincetown while I ran their company for the summer.

"Tom, I have been working like a Mexican busboy all summer long, and haven't had time to meet anyone," I said. "I haven't gotten laid in like six months. This is pathetic."

"I know," Michael chimed in. "Why don't we set him up with James?"

"Who the fuck is James?" Tom asked.

"You know," Michael said, "*James*"

Tom's eyes lit up. "Oh yea, James!"

"James? Who is James? Will I like him?" I asked, clamoring for anyone to pay the slightest bit of attention to me.

"James is this fabulous guy we met in Provincetown this summer. I think you will really like him," Michael said as he smiled at Tom.

"What does he look like?" I asked.

"You know," Michael said, "he's cute."

"Ok, what does he do for a living?" I asked.

"You know, I don't remember, but he's really successful."

"Ok, well, when can I meet him?"

"I will have to find out. He is really busy, but I will let you know by the end of the week."

I was so excited about my potential date that I had to call someone.

"Hey, Mom," I said into my cell, "Tom and Michael have this fabulous friend that they are really pumped for me to meet. He may be the one!"

The week passed and Michael called me and told me that James wanted to meet me at a bar on Bleeker Street called Alibi. I have never heard of such a place but went there in hopes I was meeting my future baby's daddy. I was really looking forward to this blind date. I had never been on a blind date before and thought that it may be a good way to at least hook up. Tom and Michael were two of my best friends so surely they would know who a good match for me would be. Perhaps this James fellow was the one.

I got to Alibi a few moments early and stood outside of the bar and smoked two cigarettes and read the latest Soap Opera Digest. It is a ritual of mine every Wednesday to pick up the new Digest after work and read it cover to cover. It's Mark time. Time for me to relax and catch up with the week's events. I hoped that James liked soaps. If not, he would have to be dumped immediately. Suddenly I remembered a few years earlier when my first boyfriend told me that I needed to stop watching my shows because it was ruining our relationship. I told him that I had watched my stories twenty years before he came along and that I would be watching them for the next twenty so he needed to get used to it. Clearly, that didn't work, as I was now going on a blind date so obviously I was going to have to take a new approach to the dating scene. I glanced down at my watch and saw that it was almost time for James to meet me, so I ducked into the bar and sat on a bar stool. I waited for a few more minutes until the person I assumed was James came into the bar. A twenty-something with a red Jew-Fro, a beer belly and a touch of the Downs sashayed his way into the bar, looking disheveled and out of breath.

"You Mark?" James asked me as he threw the twenty bags he had carried into the bar down onto the floor.

Could I fake my own death and get out of this blind date or did I have to move forward with this?

"Maybe," I replied.

"Good," James said as he stuck his hand out to meet mine. I shook his hand and could feel the sweat dripping from it. What in the hell were Tom and Michael thinking setting me up with this guy? I know it had been a slow summer, but surely they thought I had better taste than this. Having remembered to never judge a book by its cover, I decided to have a few drinks with him. If nothing else, I could get a good buzz and possibly a nice conversation out of it. The bartender walked over to greet us.

"Hi. Can I get you a –."

"Cosmopolitan," I said, cutting her off.

"Hmmm," James said. "Do you have cran-apple juice?"

I looked at him as if he had just asked for a Big Mac at a steakhouse.

"Excuse me?" the bartender said.

"Do you have cran-apple juice?" James asked again.

"Ummm…no," the bartender said. "We have cranberry juice if you'd like that."

James threw his hands up in the air in disgust.

"What are you four years old? Who the hell even drinks cran-apple juice? Why don't you just get a drink drink?" I asked.

"I don't drink," he replied. Well, that was Strike One as far as I was concerned. I don't trust anyone who doesn't drink. Actually, it was more like Strike Three if I counted his offensive looks and the awful way he was treating the bartender. "I'll just have water."

The bartender walked away and made my Cosmo and got James his water. I decided to move forward and try to be nice to the awful man that sat before me. Perhaps I had not gotten laid in six months because of my own terrible attitude. Maybe if I tried being nice to this monster, it would pay off for me in the long run.

"So, what do you do?" I asked.

James sighed, "I work in IT and I hate it. Everyone there is so obnoxious. I don't know how I deal with it on a daily basis. They are always complaining about everything and I am the only one there with a personality."

"*Really?*" I asked in surprise.

"Yes," James replied. "What I really want to do is move into customer service. I think I am a people person. Don't you?"

I thought he was joking, but wasn't sure so I just didn't answer.

"What do you do?" James asked.

"Oh, I work for Tom and Michael."

"Who?"

The bartender came back with our drinks. She sat the cosmopolitan I ordered in front of me and I grasped it. I put it to my lips and chugged as much as I could without looking like a complete alcoholic. When the bartender walked away, James pulled me close to him and whispered in me ear: "Let's get her fired."

"What?" I said as I pulled away from him, "why would we do that?"

"Because she was giving me attitude."

"Dude, you ordered a cran-apple juice. This is a bar, not the elementary school cafeteria. I would have given you attitude if you asked me for that."

"Whatever, I think she was being rude."

I couldn't take it anymore. I excused myself for a second and walked outside to smoke a quick cigarette and call Tom. Had Tom and Michael gone completely insane? Certainly James and I were not a good fit. How could we be? He was a total mess. I picked up my cell and dialed Tom's number, but it went straight to voicemail.

"Damn it Tom!" I yelled into his voicemail box. "What the hell is wrong with you? Is this some sort of joke? I cannot believe that you set me up with this reject. I am going to *kill you!*" I dragged the remains of my cigarette and walked back into the bar. I sat down next to James and he looked at me as if I had just told him he had cancer and was going to die by the end of our meeting.

"Those people," James said as he glanced behind him and gestured to the people sitting at the table against the wall. "Those people were eavesdropping on our conversation."

"What conversation? I just stepped outside," I replied.

"Before you left, I mean," he replied.

"I don't think so, and who cares anyway? We weren't talking about anything important."

"Excuse me!" James said as he got up from his stool and walked toward the couple sitting at the table against the wall. "Is there something I can help you with?"

"What are you talking about?" the woman said.

"You were eavesdropping on our conversation," James said.

"No, we weren't," the woman, replied.

"Yes, you were. I don't appreciate it either. My friend and I were having a private conversation and I would really like it if you didn't listen in."

I sat on my bar stool and was more embarrassed than I had even been in my life. Between the juice and blowing up at the bartender and the patrons of the bar, I was beginning to question just how desperate I really was. Why had I sat through this nightmare of a date for as long as I had? I got up from my barstool and grabbed James.

"James," I said trying my best to look sick, "I am really not feeling well all of the sudden. I need to go."

"Why?" he asked, "I thought we were having a really nice time."

"Well…" I said, "It's just suddenly, I feel ill." I was going to be sick if I have to continue on with this date.

"Please stay," he said.

I felt bad for the guy. He was just so utterly clueless.

"I am sorry," I said, "but I really need to go…now."

"Please stay," he asked again.

I gestured toward the bartender to come over so I could pay my check and get the hell out of there as soon as possible, but she was ignoring me. Perhaps we should have gotten her fired after all. James continued begging me to stay until I finally slapped a twenty-dollar bill on the bar, clutched the martini glass and knocked the remains of my cosmopolitan into my mouth. I slammed the martini glass down on the bar and turned around to leave.

As I was walking out the door, James asked me again, "Mark, are you sure you want to leave?"

"YES!" I yelled.

"Well, that's a shame," James said. "Because if you had stayed for four more minutes, you would have won one-hundred dollars, because you are on MTV's hidden camera-show 'Boiling Points.'"

I turned around and began laughing so hard I could not control myself.

Suddenly, Tom and Michael as well as two cameramen appeared out of nowhere.

"You've got to be fucking kidding me with this right now," I said.

"We got you!" Tom said as he laughed.

"Oh My God!" I said. I was so shocked.

"We watched the whole thing from behind the bar!" Michael said, "You were hilarious!"

"You're such a moron," Tom said, "but you look damn good on TV."

"You fuckers got me!" I said.

Apparently, when Michael had been bored a few weeks ago, he went on craigslist looking for something though I am not sure what. He came across an ad MTV had put out that said "Trick Your Friend and Make Money Doing It."

"I knew you were desperate enough to fall for it!" Michael said.

"Thanks," I replied.

James came over to me and apologized for being such an asshole. He told me that he was an actor and that his real name wasn't James, but Peter and that he had been doing the show for over a year. Suddenly, James/Peter became attractive to me. When he wasn't acting like a complete mess, he was kind of a gentleman, but, alas, he had a boyfriend. I figured I might as well ask since I did not win a hundred dollars and still hadn't gotten laid. James/Peter made me sign a consent form so that MTV could air it on television. I gladly signed it; after all, they really had gotten me.

As we were leaving the bar, my mother called, most likely to see how the date was going.

"So?" my mother said into the phone.

I replied: "Have I got a story for you…"

HAPPY NEW YEAR!!!

"2006 is going to be the breast year ever!" I yelled as 2005 came to a close and the promise of better times lie ahead.

"You said BREAST! ha, ha, ha" my friend Sally said as we embraced and rang the New Year in.

2005 was a stressful year for everyone. I had started a new job that I was totally under qualified for so pretending to know what I was doing on a daily basis was taxing to say the least. I was also in the home stretch of my six-year foray in college. Having only one semester left, I began to worry that I would not have being in college as an excuse anymore to get shit faced drunk all the time. Luckily, I realized that my creativity would eventually pay off where that was concerned. "It's May Day! Let's get wasted!" I proclaimed on Tuesday May 1st of that year. I later learned that any excuse is in fact a good excuse to drink.

New Year's of 2006 was quite a shit show. A group of friends and I had gone to some girl's apartment building and rang in the New Year on her rooftop overlooking the Empire State Building. It was a magical evening. As the party eventually died down, a group of us decided to head down to the West Village to our favorite piano bar. It was perfect for me, because I had just moved into a fabulous new duplex in the village and would only be blocks away from home when it came time to pass out. I had predicted a blackout early in the evening, so the closer I was to my bed, the easier it would be for me to navigate my journey. I had all but perfected the fastest route from the piano bar back to my apartment so heading down the village that night was prefect.

My friends and I got to the piano bar and all was well. We had a blast and everything from *Gypsy* to *My Fair Lady* was sung as we laughed and drank. I was so optimistic about what the New Year had to offer that I guess I got carried away and had one too many drinks. I was nearing a blackout when I decided to bid my friends adieu and head home. However, before I did anything, I was going to have to use the bathroom because I had just chugged four beers and really needed to pee. I went down to the bathroom at the piano bar and noticed it was ten deep. I figured it would take me just as long to walk home and use my own bathroom so I ran out of the piano bar and began my walk up Seventh Avenue en route to my place.

It was a rainy evening and the drops of water hitting the pavement, reminded me of having to pee. I was only about five blocks away from home, but with every step I took, the more I needed to pee. Suddenly I flashed back to when I was in the sixth grade and for some odd reason all of the bathrooms in my school were locked and I ended up peeing my pants. Unfortunately, as I was hustling down the avenue that was the only image I could remember until I finally stopped dead in my tracks.

"What if I just pee my pants?" I asked myself aloud. Then I remembered that I had moved into this fabulous new duplex apartment with two strangers and they did not know the heights my alcoholism could reach. I had only lived with these girls for two months and I did not think that they were ready to experience my drunken shenanigans firsthand, even though a week beforehand, I found one of my roommates passed out drunk in the hallway with her key still in the door. As I contemplated what to do, I peed my pants.

"Damn it!" I screamed. I was in a brand new suit and was standing at the corner of Seventh Avenue and Charles Street pissing myself. It was already coming out, so I just went with it. Once it starts, there really is no reason to stop it. As the pee warmed my legs and went into my shoes, I continued walking up the street. A homeless man glared at me with a look that said, *Oh yea, I've been there before.* I was so embarrassed to be seen by anyone. I began walking briskly in my piss soaked clothes until I reached my apartment. I had hoped that my roommates would be asleep as it was now four in the morning, but I noticed that one of my roommate's lights were on.

"Mother fucker!" I yelled. My roommate was such a Chatty Cathy that I knew she would want to come out of her room and go over the evenings events while we braided each others' hair. I had to find a way to cover up the fact that I had peed all over myself, but how? Then I realized that I could create an elaborate lie to get myself out of this mess. That never fails. I took a nosedive into the biggest puddle on the street, walked up the steps and into my apartment, dripping wet.

"Oh my God Mark, what happened to you?" my roommate said as I entered the door.

I fell onto the hallway floor after entering the apartment and laid spread eagle, "You'll never imagine the night I've had," I said grasping for air.

"Are you OK?" my roommate asked.

"Man," was all I could come up with.

"What?"

"A man," I said, "a man tried to RAPE ME!"

"What?" my roommate said, "are you OK? We have to call the police!"

"No!" I screamed as I leapt to my feet. "I mean, I *think* he was trying to rape me. Or mug me. I am not sure."

"Mark, we have to call the police," my roommate said. "What if he followed you home?"

"No, I am sure he didn't."

My roommate gave me the once over and noticed that I was soaking wet. "Why are you all wet?"

"Well," I said, gasping for air. I had smoked about two and a half packs of cigarettes and drank about forty beers, so I was in no condition for all of this physical activity. Creating an elaborate web of lies on the other hand, I was totally up for. "I was walking home from the bar. A bunch of us were out for New Years, and I was walking home alone and I noticed that someone was following me. Every time I began to walk faster, he picked up his speed. I was getting really scared so I began running and he came running after me." I still had not thought of any excuse for being soaked to the bone so I paused.

"And…?"

"Well, the only thing I could think to do was to play dead. So I fell into the biggest puddle I saw and pretended to be dead. You know, like those goats in Ireland do."

My roommate gave me a look that could kill. She knew something had to be up, "Why did you think he was going to rape you?"

"He had rape in his eyes!" I yelled.

"So, you saw what he looked like?"

"No," I replied, "only his eyes. His rape filled eyes."

"Mark, I think you need to go to bed. It looks like you've had a long night."

And with that, it was over. If only I was fucking wasted and pissed myself was a good excuse for my behavior, this conversation would have never taken place. I figured conjuring up a faux rape story was a lot easier than telling my roommate that I had pissed myself on the way home from a bar.

Turns out 2006 wasn't the breast year after all. After a start like that, it was not surprising.

GREETINGS FROM OUR NATION'S C(R)APITOL!!!

After eight fun-filled years in New York, I hopped on a train headed toward to D.C., my hometown. I had tried to make it work in New York for years, but after a slew of bad decisions, I felt it was time to get back to my roots and spend some time with my family. It was a last minute decision to move back to our nation's capitol, but I felt it was the right one to make. I knew that D.C. did not compare in any way to New York, but I always remember people going out to Happy Hour after work and drinking way too much. If everyone drank like that, I knew I would fit right in. But after only a few short weeks, I found myself regretting the decision to come home and wondering what crack I had been smoking that made me think moving from Varsity (New York) back to Junior Varsity (D.C.) was a good idea. For a year, my experiences in D.C. were like nothing else I had encountered before. It was like I had gotten on a train and taken it to another world, a world where no one made sense but me. Please join me as I take you, gentle reader, on a journey through my shenanigans in our great nation's crapitol.

A few days after moving back to D.C., my sister Kim told me that her office was hiring. She worked at a dating agency in Farragut Square on Connecticut Avenue and K Street. It was the most popular dating agency in the D.C. Metro area called It's Just Lunch. The premise of It's Just Lunch is that people come in and are interviewed by one of the representatives and asked questions about their lives and what they are looking for in a mate. Then a coordinator matches the person with someone they think will be a good match for them. The dates are completely blind, and people meet at bars and restaurants in an area that accommodates both parties. Neither party is told what the other looks like and the host at the bar or restaurant they meet at, shows each person to their date. The next day both parties call back and give feedback on their date and whether or not they want to see said person again. It's pretty basic, but It's Just Lunch had many success stories of people meeting, getting married and even having children. When my sister told me that there was a position there, I jumped on it, since I had no other prospects having just returned from New York.

"It sounds pretty lame," I told my sister.

"It's a job, and it can be pretty fun," Kim said with a smile. "Some of these people are so socially retarded, it's hilarious."

I went in for an interview and was offered the job on the spot. Having nothing else to do, and little money, I took it. The first few days were fun. I enjoyed coordinating random stranger's dates for them. I took pleasure in knowing that I could be setting up the next It's Just Lunch success story. The thing is D.C. is notorious for having far more women then men, so the men at the dating service pretty much got pimped out. We would set a guy up with one really hot woman and then send him out on a date with three really awful women and the cycle would continue.

"Hey, Rick, it's Mark calling from It's Just Lunch" I would say into the phone. "How did your date with Cynthia go?"

"It was awesome!" Rick replied, "Cynthia is amazing, she is everything I ever wanted in a woman." Meaning, she was hot and did not have any children.

"Well, I am certainly glad you liked her, are you ready to meet your next date?"

"I kind of wanted to see how things went with Cynthia."

"Well Rick, you know the deal. Until you go on hold, we continue to set you up on dates," I replied.

"Did Cynthia go on hold?" Rick asked. Members were allowed to put their account "on hold" to see how things went with a particular date.

"No," I replied.

DAMN THAT BITCH he was probably thinking.

"Ok, tell me about this next girl," he said, defeated, in hopes the next girl would put out faster than Cynthia.

"Well, Sandy is fantastic and I think you are really going to love her," I said. As I looked down at Sandy's file, I could tell Rick, the high-powered attorney with seventy mile an hour hair and a smile for days was not going to like Sandy at all. Sandy was forty two (Rick's age limit was thirty-five, even though he was a "young fifty." She was a bit heavy, while Rick was looking for someone athletic. Sandy also had buckteeth.) But, Sandy was a customer at It's Just Lunch and like everyone else; she was entitled to her one date a month. Having just set Rick up with Cynthia, who was fabulous, he owed me a favor. "Sandy is a schoolteacher," I said into the phone, "she loves dogs, and has one of her own. She also loves the beach just like you."

"Does she work out?" Rick asked.

I looked at Sandy's picture and glanced at her double chin: "It doesn't say, but I would say from her picture, she's been to the gym a few times in her life." A few times being the key words.

"Ok, is she blonde?"

"Rick, you know we cannot really tell you what your dates look like. It's Just Lunch policy clearly states that we are not supposed to describe what your dates look like before you meet them. You came up as a match on the computer," which was a total lie. There was no computer. We would pull people's files out from the drawer and I would decide whether or not I thought they would make a cute baby together, "I am simply telling you about your next date, so please let's follow protocol."

"Ok, Mark, you're such a stickler for following the rules." I really wasn't, but after being on the phone all day with these people repeating myself over and over again, I used the 'protocol' excuse to get them off my back.

"Thanks, Rick. So why don't you guys meet at…" I trailed off. The hardest part of arranging dates for me was figuring out where these people should meet. I had not lived in D.C. for very long, and to be honest I had no idea where I was half the time, let alone where these people's offices were. "So, you work on Capitol Hill, right?" I asked.

"Yes," he said.

"Ok, she works in Friendship Heights, so where would be good in the middle? Arlington?"

"That's in Virginia, I don't really think that would work out."

Damn it, "Dupont Circle?"

"Sure, I can meet in Dupont," he replied. I would pretty much just rattle off neighborhoods until someone would tell me one that worked for them.

"Ok, Dupont Grille it is. How about 7:30 tomorrow night?"

"Ok."

"Ok, remember to check in with hostess when you get there and she will make sure that you find Sandy. Have a good time." I hung up.

Now it was time to call Sandy.

"Sandy, it's Mark from It's Just Lunch."

"Oh, hello," Sandy said into the phone. I had only spoken to her a few times before, but she was sweet, like schoolteachers are supposed to be.

"Have I got a date for you!"

I continued to rattle on and on about Rick and how I thought they were a perfect match. Deep inside, I knew it would never work out for them. Rick was a pig, as most men are and was only worried about what people looked like. Sandy was sweet and seemed almost naïve in her forty-two years of age. I got Sandy really pumped for the date and told her to wear something slutty, which is totally against the rules. I figured Sandy was entitled to get laid, just like the rest of us and if she wore something a little skimpier, it would at least increase her odds.

The exchange between the two parties and making reservations at the restaurant where they were to meet would take about an hour. Afterwards, I would smoke a cigarette and try to hustle magazines from the Persian woman at the deli downstairs.

After a few weeks, I was really getting the hang of things, but one thing really bothered me. One of my clients, Marc K., who I thought was totally cute was not having any luck getting second dates.

"Any luck with Gretchen?" I asked after his date.

"No. I haven't heard back from her," Marc said.

"I wonder why," I said. He was so cute, in that nerdy, computer repairman kind of way. I looked into his file and looked at the picture in it. He was about my height, five feet, eight inches tall. He had short brown hair and the cutest little glasses. I had to find him a date. "Listen Marc, I am really invested in finding you 'the one,'" I said, "I don't know why but I feel a connection to you, and feel that maybe I need to give you some pointers at getting you that second date." I felt a connection to him, because I secretly wanted to date him myself, but I had absolutely no idea what appropriate blind date etiquette was. The last blind date I went on, I had gotten totally wasted and ended up making out with the bartender at the restaurant where I had met my blind date.

"Could you help me?" Marc asked.

It was totally against the rules, but I figured, what the hell? If he ends up getting married in a few months to the woman of his dreams then everyone will be happy; and if he realizes that he is gay and wants to be with me, then it's win win for the both of us.

I met Marc one night at a bar down the street from my office. I walked up to him and introduced myself. It was like I was going on an It's Just Lunch Date of my own.

"Thanks for meeting me," my dorky new friend said. He was just so cute with his glasses. We sat down and ordered a few drinks. "Why do you think I am not meeting anyone?"

"I am not really sure, Marc . You are just as cute as you could be," I said. One beer and I was already flirting with a straight client, "what do you find interesting in a woman?"

"Their hair," he replied.

"Excuse me?"

"Their hair," he said again. "You can tell a lot about a woman by her hair." He could tell I was confused. "I don't know. You can tell if a woman is a good match by the way she presents herself and I think that a woman with good hair usually has her shit together. All of the women who you have set me up with had unmanageable hair, which means their lives must be a mess. A woman with bad hair is usually bad at life."

I didn't know how to respond so I just said, "you know what, I think you are right." After another beer and a few minutes of thinking about, I really did think Marc was right. All of the woman I knew who had unmanageable hair were messes. I remember when I was younger, my mother's hair was always a mess and Lord knows she definitely didn't have her shit together. Marc and I had a few more beers and I gave him some drunken pointers on how to get a second date. Such as, get her drunk in hopes she winds up in your bed the next morning. There's your second date. I don't know if it helped, but I felt bad for the guy. I also told him that he needed to offer to pick up the check when he took woman out for dinner.

"I have no intention of paying for a stranger's meal," he said.

"Well, if you are interested in a woman, then you need to show her your interest. Picking up the check is a nice gesture."

"But what if I never see her again? Then I have just lost nine dollars that I will never get back!" Where the hell was he taking his dates? Denny's?

"Trust me."

A few weeks later, Marc went on hold so he could date, Nancy, a girl from the service, exclusively. I think our little pep talk had something to do with it. And the fact that I told Nancy to get her hair blown out before meeting Marc probably didn't hurt either.

Not all of our clients were as easy to deal with as Marc. One woman, Rose, nearly drove me to an early grave. She was about fifty years old and weighed about fifty pounds. I don't know if she was anorexic or just skinny, but she was frightening to look at and scared the shit out of me every time we spoke on the phone. When her time for a date rolled around, I hesitated calling her, but was forced to by my precarious boss.

"Rose?" I said into the phone.

"Who the hell is this?" Rose responded.

"It's Mark from It's Just Lunch."

"Oh yeah. What's up you little fairy? You gotta date for me?"

"Ha Ha. Yea. His name is Ron."

"Is he cute? Or is he a fatty like that last guy you set me up with?" Thinking she considered any one over fifty pounds a fatty, I responded:

"No, he is fit. He's very nice. He works for the government."

"This is D.C., everyone works for the fucking government. I work for the fucking government."

"I don't work for the government."

"That's cause you're a fairy. They don't let fairies work for the fucking government."

"It's no wonder you're still single Rose, with a mouth like that."

"Whatever," she said taking a drag off her cigarette, blowing it into the phone, making me now crave a cigarette. "Where does he live?"

"Virginia."

"I'm not fucking going to Virginia."

"Rose, you know the deal. You will meet him somewhere in the middle. Maybe Dupont Circle." I had quickly realized that Dupont Circle was the middle of everything.

"Fine. Where?"

"Daily Grille?"

"I hate that fucking place!"

"Kramer's?"

"Fine."

After wondering what difference it was going to make, as she was probably not going to eat anyway, I hung up. I called Ron and told him about his date with Rose. The poor guy had no idea what I had just gotten him into. A few days later, I came to work and received one of the most horrifying messages I have ever heard:

"You fucking homo!" Rose said into my answering machine. "I cannot believe that you set me up with that big fat pig. He was so fat. You said he went to the gym. I don't think he has ever even looked at a gym, let alone walked inside one before. If I ever see you, I am going to beat the shit out of you. Have you seen my picture? I am beautiful. I cannot believe that you think I would be a good match with that piece of shit. He didn't even pay the check! I can't believe this. I am calling your boss and telling him that you should be fired! I cannot believe this. I cannot believe this. FUUUUCCCCCKKKKK!!!!!!"

Apparently she couldn't believe that I set her up with someone who didn't share the same passion for abstaining from food as she did. Shortly after, I quit It's Just Lunch. I decided I needed to focus on finding myself a boyfriend and not worry about all of these people's horrifying love lives.

I had only worked at the dating service for two and half months, but I really couldn't deal with my own life, let alone the love lives of thirty complete strangers. I read an advertisement about a gay owned company that was looking for salesman and went in for an interview. I was not really sure what I was getting myself into, but decided it would give me a chance to meet other gay guys in the area, something I had not done at that point in time. I went in for my interview and was greeted by a really nice gay guy named Mark. I guess Shirley McLaine was right; all gay guys are named Mark, Rick or Steve.

"So let me tell you a little something about what we do here," other gay Mark said. "We are like a gay phone book. We are like a one stop shop for everything gay."

"Wait a second. Gay guys in D.C. need their own phone book?" I asked.

"Well, yes," he replied.

"Why can't they just use the regular phone book?"

"Because when they use our phone book, they know that all of the stores and services are gay owned or gay friendly."

"But it's 2008. Do people even use phone books anymore?"

For someone trying to get a job, I was certainly asking a lot of unnecessary questions.

"Yes, in D.C. they do," other gay Mark, replied.

I was quickly realizing that D.C. was even more backwards than I thought it was. People in D.C. were like ten years behind what everyone in New York was doing.

"For example," other gay Mark continued, "this cupcake store is in our book," as he pointed to an ad in the gay phone book. "But the other one, right across the street, isn't. So, if you are a gay consumer, you would be more inclined to use the cupcake store that was in our book than the other one."

"Why are there so many cupcake stores in D.C.?" I asked.

"I don't know."

"Because, you know, the whole cupcake fad has come and gone in New York," I replied.

"Well cupcakes are very hot in D.C. right now," he said.

After an hour-long conversation about cupcakes and gay guys, I left the office. A few days later, other gay Mark called and told me that I had somehow gotten the job. I wasn't really sure what I was going to be doing, but I am always down for a new adventure. To celebrate, I called my friend Jonathon, who I met when I was in college, who happened to live in D.C.

"I am so glad you are in D.C. We are going to have so much fun," Jonathon said into the phone.

"Sure," I replied unenthusiastically.

"C'mon Mark, you have to give D.C. a chance. I know it is not New York, but it's fun here."

"Really?" I asked with sarcasm.

"Yes. In fact, we are going into Town tonight. It's a disco-boutique."

"What?"

"A disco-boutique."

"What does that even mean? That's totally an oxymoron. It doesn't even make sense."

"It's a club Mark. Just come with us. It will be like a *Mean Girls* reunion!" Jonathon has this warped idea that he is Regina George from *Mean Girls*. Our friend Chris is Karen, because he is the dumb blonde one and I am Gretchen because I am the Jew.

"Ok, I'll come with you," I said.

That evening, Jonathon, Chris and I went to the disco-boutique a.k.a. the only gay club in D.C. and danced and had a gay old time. It was a fun club, but I couldn't help but notice that no one came up to talk to Jonathon, Chris or myself. We had a great time with each other, but it was as if everyone else kept to themselves. In New York, people seemed to be much friendlier, everyone mingled and had a good time and met new people. In D.C., it seemed as though *Mean Girls* had actually come to life. Everyone was in their own clique and no one mingled with anyone else. It seemed so juvenile that everyone ignored everyone else. Little did I know, this is how they roll in D.C. and I would soon find out just how awful it actually was.

The following Monday, I began my job at the gay phone book. It was the easiest job I had ever had. All I had to do was make phone calls and take clients out to lunch and tell them that advertising in the gay phone book would increase their business. All I did was bullshit my way through which is pretty much my specialty so the job was a perfect fit.

By the time spring rolled around, drinking season began. It seemed as though the second the temperature went above fifty degrees, everyone was out drinking and having a good old time. I quickly realized that D.C. residents were just about the laziest group of people in America. Everyone left his or her office at 5pm on the dot to go to Happy Hour every single night. No one worked late. In New York, everyone worked until at least six, if not later and no one really went to Happy Hour. While I was happy to see a potential for a ton of new drinking buddies, I was concerned that I was the only one in the city with the slightest bit of work ethic.

As the weather continued to amaze, my social calendar quickly began to fill up. Through Jonathon, I had met a few new friends. I didn't really like any of them because they were very fake towards me, but I went along with them because I really had no other option since I didn't have any friends of my own. One particular April evening, Jonathon gave me a call:

"Hey, Mark, I was invited to a sick party tonight. There are going to be a lot of super hot guys there."

"Really? Where is it?"

"The Diner on 18th Street," he replied.

"Why are they having a party at a diner?"

"I don't know; it's just what they do."

"And who exactly are *they*?"

"A.O.F."

"Abercrombie and Fitch?"

"No you dumbass," Jonathon said, "Axis of Fun."

I laughed so loud that everyone in my big gay office could hear, "what the hell is the Axis of Fun?"

"It's like a fraternity," he continued, "they are a group of really successful gay guys that created a group called the Axis of Fun. They throw a bunch of parties every year at the Diner. It's a really exclusive invite. We should totally go."

"If they are like a fraternity, do they do community service?"

"No."

"So what exactly is the point?"

"Mark, why are you always looking for answers for everything?"

"Because the Axis of Fun is just about the most ridiculous thing I have ever heard of. I mean, the name alone is hilarious: Axis of Fun." I laughed so hard I almost peed.

"But I really want to be a member, we have to go."

"Why? It sounds like these kids were rejects in high school and decided to make a group up to make themselves feel better."

"Whatever. You don't have to go."

"Now, I *have* to go so I can see this shit show for myself."

That night, Jonathon and I went to the party that the Axis of Fun was hosting at the Diner. The Diner is a really cute place, after all. It is green and orange on the outside and looks like a drag queen threw up all over it. Inside, there is a chandelier made of martini glasses and posters of New Jersey everywhere. I really liked the décor; the clientele on the other hand, was another story. Jonathon and I stood in the corner and were ignored, just as we had been at the disco-boutique. After about four martinis and Jonathon's mysterious disappearance to the bathroom for hours, I decided I would try to strike up a conversation with someone. Maybe gay people in D.C. were just socially awkward and needed someone to throw out a conversation topic for them.

"Hey," I said as I walked over to a guy standing in a suit and tie by himself in the corner.

"Oh, hello," he said, "my name is Andrew, what's yours?"

"I'm Mark," I said, "pretty lame party, huh?"

"Well…" he said as I cut him off.

"I don't understand why this whole A.O.F. thing is anyway. Oh well. Are you a member?"

"Actually, I founded A.O.F."

"Oh," I said as I slowly walked backwards.

"Do you have a problem with it?" he asked.

"No."

"Good, I didn't think so." Andrew walked away. So much for trying to make friends in D.C.

I stood in the corner by myself for about an hour before Jonathon resurfaced. I had nothing to do but drink and managed to polish off at least half a bottle of vodka by myself.

"Finally, where have you been?" I asked.

"Making out with the hottest guy in the bathroom," he replied.

"Jesus, Jonathon let's go," I cried, "I have already made an ass out of myself once tonight, I would really rather not do it again."

"Well you can go, I am staying." I had no idea how to get home. D.C. was still a labyrinth to me, and I had not yet figured out how to get from place to place without a guide. When I was a kid, I was chaperoned around so I never bothered figuring out how to get from place to place. Now I was on my own. I had to stay or take the chance of getting lost on my way home. I continued standing in the corner alone, until someone walked up to talk to me.

"Hi," the guy said, "my name is Chuck."

"Mark," I replied. Having already embarrassed myself in front of the A.O.F.'s I decided short, to the point answers were all anyone was getting out of me.

"What do you do for a living?" I had only been in D.C. for four months, but I had already figured out that people would introduce themselves and follow the introduction by asking what your profession was. It's protocol in these parts.

"I work for the gay phone book."

"Really? I use that thing all the time. It's a great service," Chuck said.

"*Really?*" I asked quizzically. Having not used a phone book since I was in middle school to prank call the rape hotline, I was shocked by his response.

"Yes, all the time. Every business I frequent, I found from the gay phone book."

"Wow," I said, wondering what all of my cool friends in New York were doing. "What do you do?"

"I work on the Hill." This was a typical response to this question. All "power gays" in D.C. work on the Hill. The first time someone had told me they worked on the Hill, I misunderstood them and thought that they worked on the TV show *The Hills*. Much to my disappointment, they meant Capitol Hill.

"Oh, what do you do on the Hill?" I asked.

"I work for a Republican Senator from Tennessee," he replied.

"Really?"

"Yes."

"You work for a Republican? But you're gay, right?"

"Yes."

"Then, why do you work for someone who is totally against everything you believe in?"

"It's a job. I want to work in politics, so I have to make concessions. He does not know I am gay, so it's totally ok."

"Even if he did know you were gay, it would still be OK. He can't fire you because you are gay. Are you even a Republican?"

"Yes."

"Really? Why?" Chuck fascinated me. He was everything I never wanted to be.

"Because I believe in the Republican way of dealing with finances in the government."

"What about your basic human rights? Most Republicans don't really like gays."

"That's not true."

"Dick Cheney doesn't even like his own daughter and she's a big fucking dyke!"

"It's not true, there are a lot of Republicans who are gay-friendly."

"Just because they are gay-friendly doesn't mean they will ever support gay-rights."

Chuck looked at me with anger. I guess no one had ever called him out on his bullshit before. It absolutely amazed me that this guy would go around pretending to be something he is not to get a job, working for someone who would most likely rather see him dead than alive. No one in New York ever pretended to be something that they weren't. Except rich. Everyone pretends to be rich in New York, but that's status quo.

"I don't really want to have this conversation right now," Chuck said as he walked away. I was not having a good time making friends in this city. I knew that the best way to feel bad about yourself was to be in a room filled with gay men, but nothing had prepared me for this. I couldn't believe the ridiculous shit that went on in D.C. The gay phone book, the AOF, the gay Republicans. I couldn't find Jonathon so I left without him. I couldn't be in a room with these people any longer. I had to walk home by myself and it took me an hour because I got lost seven times.

"That's what you get for hanging out with a bunch of homos!" my co-worker Andre said the next day. Andre was the graphic designer for the gay phone book and was one of the most racist, homophobic black gay guys I had ever met. "You know, the gay guys down here really need to their priorities straight," he continued, "they had to lay off half of the staff at the AIDS clinic down the street due to lack of donations. But, the gays down here have enough money to throw a gay pride pet parade. They threw a God damned gay pride for their pets. What the fuck is that about?"

As I listened I sat with my head on my desk. How was I supposed to make it work in D.C.? People down here were from another breed, I really did not know if I was ever going to fit in. In New York, crazy people are crazy; shady people are shady and assholes are assholes. In D.C., it seemed as though everyone was fake but made you think they were your friend before they talked shit about you behind your back then give you their business card and told you to call them. I wasn't sure how long I was going to make it.

"And as far as the A.O.F. goes," Andre continued, "that's just typical D.C. homo bullshit. I wouldn't let it bother you. You're better than that."

He was right I was better than that. Who did these homos think they were? I lived in New York for eight years. All of these boys had come from the back woods of Kentucky and West Virginia where no one liked them because they were socially awkward. Now, they were in the "big city" and thought that their shit didn't stink because they worked on Capitol Hill and made twenty-nine thousand dollars a year. Well,

I had a news flash for all of them. I came from New York, which automatically made eight million other people and me, cooler than anyone that lived in D.C. After only having lived in D.C. for a few months, I was already ready to move. D.C. was not for me as I hate politics and that's all anyone seemed to talk about. It was as if no one had a life of his or her own. Everything revolved around something else. Politics, occupations, other people's gossip and problems, it was as if no one had anything important to say. Never was I at a loss for conversation in New York. Everyone is so colorful and has a story to tell up there. As I left work that day, I was planning my getaway. I figured if I had spent just a few more weeks in D.C., and saved some money, I could leave and never come back. As I was plotting my escape, I was walking up 18th street toward Adams Morgan. Adams Morgan is a neighborhood in D.C. that must be what the eighth circle of hell is like. Every night, underage college kids congregate in Adams Morgan to get black out drunk and make complete asses of themselves. It's a constant shit show, with girls throwing their brains up on the street, frat boys getting into petty fights over girls and pimps whoring out their latest prizes. It's an absolutely disgusting display of what the bottom wrung of humanity looks like, but it was on my way to the subway and I had to get home immediately to plot my escape from D.C.

I walked up the hill to get to the top of 18th street so I could get on the subway. To my left, I saw two bitches in tight tube-tops squawking about how one of them had stolen the other's boyfriend. In front of me, I saw the lights of the bars in Adams Morgan. I hoped to bypass this neighborhood completely, but the other Metro station was broken, as usual, so I had no choice.

As I was walking up the street, I was suddenly shoved down onto the concrete. My forehead hit the pavement and my nose smashed up against the curb. Two men came in front of me and started kicking me in the stomach repeatedly. I could not get up so I just tried to cover my face. After all, it is the moneymaker. I could taste blood in my mouth.

Just as quickly as the beating had started, the men were finished and ran away. I lay on the pavement in pain, wondering if anyone was around to help me. Strangely, it was as if everyone around me had disappeared. No longer were the slutty girls fighting over a guy; the pimps and whores had vanished and I was alone. I got up, with blood dripping from my nose and face. Of course, the one night I leave my rape whistle at home is the night I get mugged. I began to scream for help. I could see that there were cops across the street giving parking tickets but either they could not hear me, or did not want to help me. I had to get help from someone and I didn't know what to do. As I walked up the street, I began screaming for someone to help me.

"HELP ME!!!" I yelled, but no one listened. Everyone just went about their business. After screaming that D.C. sucked and everyone who lived there was going to hell for not helping me, I decided to do what I do best: ruin it for everyone. I knew from experience that all bars and restaurants are, by law, required to have first aid kits. So, with my face dripping with blood, I entered the first restaurant I saw. As I entered, I could see horror in the diner's faces. Everyone stopped eating and looked up to see me, battered and bruised. I yelled for someone to help me, and a lesbian barkeep came around from the bar and took me into the back room. I told her what had happened and she tended to me. She took the piece of glass that was stuck in my forehead out, bandaged my nose, which was broken, and cleaned the blood off of me as best she could. She was so sweet, and had I not been in such a rage, I would have been a bit nicer.

"Everyone in D.C. should die and go to hell!" I yelled at the lesbian barkeeps face.

"You must be a New Yorker," she said.

"Yes, I am, and shit like this never happens in New York. People look out for each other. I was walking up the street and no one would help me."

'This is a rough neighborhood, hun," she said as she continued to bandage my face.

"Had I not walked into your restaurant looking like the Bride of Frankenstein, no one would have helped me," I cried.

"It's ok honey."

I was sobbing like a baby that had just been thrown against a wall. The lesbian barkeep took such good care of me. When I finally left her restaurant, I told her that she was pretty nice for a lesbian and that I would be back to spend a lot of money on booze in a few weeks. But when I did eventually go back, the restaurant was closed. I guess that's what you get for being a caring, good-natured lesbian in D.C.

I walked home that night, bandaged and very angry. After each step I took another obscenity flew out of my mouth.

"FUCK EVERYONE!!!" I yelled until I made it to the subway. I went home and didn't go into work for the next week. I was bruised and swollen, with a broken nose and a broken spirit.

After a week in seclusion, I finally went back to work. The gays at the gay phone book were really nice and thoughtful and felt awful about what happened. Of course, Andre had to chime in about what happened:

"It was probably a bunch of fucking black guys," he said, "Typical."

"But you're black, why would you say that?" I asked.

"Because all of the crime in D.C. is usually linked to black people. All they do is create problems."

"Ok," I replied. After a few minutes back at the office, other gay Mark pulled me into the office and told me that the gay phone book was going through a series of pay cuts because business was not doing well. I guess the gay guys in D.C. finally realized that they could go online and get any information they needed with the click of a button instead of using a phone book. I told him I understood and that they were just doing what they needed to do to survive, but I was going to have to get a part time job in order to make ends meet. I was never going to be able to get out of D.C. after taking such a huge pay cut, so I began looking for jobs.

I found an advertisement in the paper for a restaurant down the street that was hiring. It was a small French café with a patio, located at the bottom of 18th street right next to the infamous Diner. I had my doubts about ever walking down 18th street again, but I really needed a job so I took my chances. I went in for my interview and was greeted by one of the most fabulously flamboyant men I had ever met. He was tall and extremely thin with a large head and spiky highlighted hair.
"I'm Jim," he said as he greeted me. We introduced ourselves and sat down so he could interview me. "I see you are from New York. I am too! What made you move to D.C.?"

"I really don't know," I responded.

"Not taking to D.C. are we?" he asked.

"Not really. I find people down here boring and pretentious. I am not really sure why everyone has such a huge stick up their ass, but I am trying to get used to it."

He laughed: "Yeah, I hate it here too, but my partner and I really wanted to open a French bistro and it was just too expensive to do in New York, so we decided to move down here."

"Do you like it?" I asked.

"No," Jim said, "but I love this restaurant, and I try to get out of town about once a month."

"Well, I can see why you like your restaurant," I said as I looked around. The café was cute, if nothing else. There were several chairs around several round tables scattered throughout the café. In the center, there was a huge oak bar with a brick wall behind it. Colors danced against the glasses behind the bar as 80's music played in the background. I looked up and noticed a huge disco ball hanging from the ceiling.

"What's with the disco ball?"

"Well," Jim said, "We've been known to get down here after hours."

"Really?" I asked as my eyes lit up.

"Yes. I dance on the bar and put on a show as everyone gets wasted. I try to keep the working environment as fun as possible."

I already liked Jim. He was a New Yorker for one, and seemed like a good time for another. After looking over my resume, Jim noticed that I worked at a bar in New York where he and his partner had gone on their first date. After we bonded over that, he told me that he was definitely going to hire me but needed to interview the other people he called in first. A few days later and told me that he would love it if I joined his team and couldn't wait for me to start.

A new chapter in my life began when I began working at the café. It gave me a chance to make friends with some really amazing people, something I had not done in the first four months of my D.C. residency. Everyone at the café had a story to tell. It was almost was if I were living in one big United Colors of Benetton ad. Everyone was so different.

There were Jim and Christopher, the eccentric, gay owners of the café. Then there was Rafal, a Polish guy who was a cook and his girlfriend Erica, who was Swedish and a barista. There was Yacouba, a cook from Niger, Samina, a server who hailed from Pakistan, and Damian, a server from Boston. Everyone got along really well and everyone who came into the café had a really good time. My first weekend at the café was a blur. That Friday night, Jim got on the bar and danced in a triangular straw hat to *Kung Fu Fighting*. Saturday, everyone on the patio got a free round of shots because the café had just gotten a good review in the Washington Post. Everyone seemed happy to work there and after a few weeks, I had fallen in love with the café. Maybe D.C. wasn't as bad as I thought it was.

A few weeks into my employ at the café, the gay phone book went from giving me a pay cut to just not paying me at all so I quit. It was the best decision to make after all. I could not work for free and if I did not have to work during the day, it would save up a lot of time for me to get drunk and work off hangovers. As spring continued, I was beginning to make real friends in D.C. and beginning to drink more than what I thought was humanly possibly. Every night after work, my co-workers and I would drink to the point of blacking out. Since I no longer had a job during the day, I did not mind drinking all night then waking up at four in the afternoon on a Wednesday to go to work.

One afternoon in May, I was waiting on a cute couple that sat in my section for about three hours drinking Bloody Marys and chatting. They were really cute so I introduced myself:

"I'm Mark. I meant to tell you that when you sat down and I took your order, but I guess I forgot."

"I'm Erin," the girl said.

"Jerry," the guy said.

"You guys look like you are having a lovely afternoon, drinking Bloody's and enjoying this fabulous weather," I said.

"Actually," Erin said, "We were just in the middle of a fight."

"Thank you for coming over and interrupting," Jerry said.

I laughed: "No problem."

"Hey," Jerry said, "You don't mind if we pull up another chair do you? My brother is coming to join us in a few minutes."

"Of course not," I said. "But I am heading out of here soon, so I might be coming to join you guys and your brother for a few drinks."

"We would love that," Jerry exclaimed. He then pulled me aside and whispered in my ear: "She's my mistress not my wife. I just wanted to clear that up for you before you sat down."

"I don't know your life," I said as I winked at him and walked away to finish cleaning up.

After I was done closing my checks, I saw that Jerry's brother joined him and Erin. He was a really good-looking guy. Tall and built, with blonde hair and a huge smile. He was totally cute so I sat down with the three of them and began chit chatting.

"I'm Mark," I said as I put my hand out to greet Jerry's brother.

"I'm Tim," he replied, "Are you new here? I have been coming here for years and I have never seen you before."

"Yes. I just moved down here from New York," I answered.

"Really?" he asked, "I lived in New York for some time. On Greenwich Avenue."

"Oh my God, I used to live on Greenwich and 12th!"

"What a coincidence," Tim said. We sat and chatted for hours. It was as if Tim and I were old friends since we shared so many of the same interests. Then suddenly Tim pulled out his Blackberry and I noticed the screen was welcoming him to soapcentral.com.

"Oh my God, tell me that your Blackberry does not automatically pull up soapcentral.com every time you turn it on," I said.

"Yea, I have it programmed to, why?" he asked.

"I love soaps. Which ones do you watch?" I was hoping he said he watched ABC soaps, because if he didn't, our friendship would be immediately over. I have no patience for anyone who watches anything other than ABC soaps.

"*All My Children* and *One Life to Live*," he answered.

All of the sudden, I pictured how I would look in my wedding dress when I walked down the aisle to meet Tim at the alter. "Oh my God, I have been watching those shows for like twenty years!" I gaily responded.

"Me too, I love it. My only wish is that they would bring Tina back to *One Life to Live*."

I smacked him. That was my one wish in life. That, and moving back to New York as soon as possible. "Oh My God, I think we are soul mates." I don't know if it was the twelve Bloody Marys or all of the gossiping about ABC soaps, but one thing led to another and Tim and I spent an hour making out in the café bathroom.

"There was something I meant to tell you," Tim said as we took a breath from making out, "I also watch *The Young and the Restless*," he said. He could see the disappointment in my face. How could he lie about something as important as soaps? Little did I know, that was the first of many deceptions on his part. I told him that I forgave him, but never to lie to me about something as crucial as that ever again.

For the next week Tim and I were inseparable. We loved all of the same things and we even shared a mutual fear of midgets. The next weekend he went away and I called him when he got back to see how his trip was but he never returned my call. I then texted him but never got a response from that either. By that Wednesday, I had all but given up hope. Perhaps Tim had been sent in a riverboat over a waterfall just as Tina had been on *One Life to Live* many years earlier. Maybe he would resurface in a few years and interrupt my wedding one-day just as Tina had done after she went missing. I put dreams of being Tim's baby's momma on the back burner. Maybe he was just a blip on the radar of my life. I was hurt that I had not heard from him, but decided I needed to refocus my attention. I was beginning to really like D.C. and had made so many new friends at the café that I loved hanging with. Maybe if I hung out with them and got drunk, that would ease my pain. I decided that week to join my sister Kim and my friend Jonathon out for drinks at the Diner, located next to the café I worked at. I had put all previous bad memories of AOF and their legion of gay evildoers behind me and went in.

Of course who was the first person that I bump into? Tim. "Oh my God, Mark, where have you been?" he asked.

I walked up to the bar where he was sitting and ordered a drink, "Here. Working. Where have you been?"

"I told you I was going out of town."

"I called and texted you and you never got back to me," I said.

"My phone wasn't working," he said as he was checking his e-mail on his phone. I looked at him as if he thought I was a complete moron. "Oh," he said, "I got a new one. But I never got your message."

"Ok," I continued, "Do you still want to get together sometime?"

"Sure. Why don't we have an *All My Children* marathon at my apartment on Saturday night? Have you watched this week?"

"Actually, no I haven't. That would be perfect."

"Ok, it's a date then!" he said. We knocked back a couple of drinks and I eagerly awaited my date on Saturday night. However, much to my chagrin, I got a text message from Tim on Saturday afternoon saying that he had to cancel our date. He was going to have an early night as he was leaving in the morning to go to New York and needed to rest up. I was so disappointed that I decided to meet up with some lesbian friends and get wasted. Shortly after, my friend Meg called and told me that she was going to her friend's birthday party and asked me if I wanted to join her. I agreed and walked over to the infamous diner, where Meg's friend's party was being held. Of course the first person I bumped into was Tim. I ignored him and went straight to the bar for a drink. About fifteen drinks later, I drunkenly confronted him:

"Why did you tell me that you were having a night in when you obviously weren't?"

"I didn't think I needed to give you a play by play of my life," Tim said.

"I thought we were friends. Why did you lie to me?"

"I don't need to tell you what I am doing every day. We aren't in a relationship and frankly, it's none of your business what I do."

"But, you made plans with me," I cried.

"We're not boyfriends," Tim said as he turned and walked away.

I had thought that we were at least friends, and I know that I didn't treat my friends with a complete disregard to their feelings. I was so annoyed by what happened, I walked down the street and noticed that Jim was sitting in the café, having a drink. I burst through the café door and sat next to him.

"What's wrong pumpkin?" Jim asked.

"Nothing," I replied as I took a sip of the drink the bartender handed me. I was in no condition to continue drinking, but I was upset and needed something to make me feel better.

"Boy problems?" Jim asked.

"Yeah."

"Who is the lucky guy?"

"This guy Tim, he hangs out next door at the Diner a lot," I said.

"Tim Tim? I know Tim. I slept with him a few months ago."

"Thanks, that's exactly what I needed to hear right now," I said as I downed the rest of my drink and walked out the door. I had finally started to like D.C. and now, I hated it even more than ever. People down here just did not operate properly. For the next few months, as the summer continued on, everything and everyone bothered me, and everyone experienced the wrath of Mark.

However, there were some very colorful characters that I waited on at the café. One afternoon, I was serving a very loud group of gay guys. I introduced myself, hoping to make some new friends,

"I'm Ryan," the kid who seemed to be the leader of the gays said, "Why don't you join us when you are done working?"

"Sure," I said. After I was done working, I sat down with Ryan and his army of skanks to have a few drinks.

"So Mark, where are you from?" Ryan asked.

"New York," I answered.

"Oh I love New York," Ryan said, "But I could never live there. Everyone is so mean."

"I don't think so. I think everyone in D.C. is mean. You are probably just bumping into other Washingtonians when you are in New York. That's the only reasonable excuse I can think of," I responded.

Ryan laughed: "So you don't like D.C.?"

"Nope. I think it's an awful place filled with awful people," I answered.

"Really? That's interesting. I don't think so," Ryan said.

"Maybe I have just been meeting the wrong people. I mean, I have a few good friends, but for the most part, people are pretty ridiculous down here," I said.

"Why do you say that?"

"Well for one thing, everyone is so interested in themselves that they don't ever want to get to know anyone or anything outside of their own bubble" I continued. "I don't care about politics and I am really not impressed with all of these homos who run around telling everyone that they work on the hill. Let me tell you something, I probably make more money waiting tables then those fuckers do and I don't have to change who I am every time I go to work. Also, everyone is so cliquey here. I don't get it. No one wants to make friends with anyone else and everyone is so stuck up." As I continued talking, the faces of Ryan and his friends went from half smiles to faces of sheer confusion, "Have you ever noticed that hot girls are always with really ugly guys? What is with that? It's like the girls down here will just settle for anyone that gives them the time of day. And the subway system is awful. For a metropolitan area, D.C.'s subway system is atrocious. It never works and something is always broken. I don't understand how the people who run it can be so incompetent that they can't even figure out how to make an elevator work. Also…"

Ryan cut me off: "Ok, I think we get the point."

Ryan and his friends looked at me with utter disgust. They loved D.C. and could not understand why I didn't. To change topics, I asked:

"So where are you guys from?"

"Florida," Ryan said.

"Alabama," gay number two said.

"Louisiana," gay number three said.

"Arkansas," gay number four said.

"Wow. Of course you like D.C. How could you know any better, being from places like that?"

"Mark, maybe you are having such a hard time finding friends because of your attitude." Ryan said. Maybe he was right. Maybe I did need an attitude adjustment. "My friends are having a party near the Archives tomorrow night. It's a fabulous apartment, and the party should be fun. Why don't you come with us? It will give you a chance to meet some new people."

I agreed to meet Ryan and his legion of skanks at the party near the Archives the next day. As I entered the upscale building, I regretted what I had worn. I had no idea what was in store for me upstairs, but judging from the lobby, my Abercrombie cut up jeans and worn out polo shirt were not going to fit in. As I exited the elevator and walked to the apartment door, I was greeted by Ryan who handed me a glass of wine and I walked onto the patio, where the other guests were. The patio was beautiful and had an amazing view of Washington. Across the street I could see the Archives and the Mall. To the left I could see the theatres and the White House. For a half a second, I kind of appreciated D.C. and it's architecture. That quickly passed as Ryan came over with one of his friends.

"Mark, this is Tony, he works at the White House," Ryan said to me, "Tony, this is Mark, he waits tables at the café down the street from my apartment."

"Ryan!" I screamed. "Is it necessary to introduce me to all of your friends like that?"

"Oh, I am sorry, I didn't know that you were so embarrassed by what you do for a living."

"I'm not," I said, "but there is a lot more to me than just being a waiter. I am also a writer and I really like Polo."

"Really?" Tony said, "I love Polo. I used to play on Cape Cod all the time."

"Oh no, I am sorry, I meant the brand Polo. You know, Ralph Lauren," I said as Tony looked at me like I was a complete moron.

Tony and I chatted for a bit, but I could tell that he was not interested in making conversation with me, as I was just a lowly waiter and could not help him advance in his career. In fact, once word got out that I was just a waiter, no one really talked to me at all. I stood on the patio of this amazing apartment wondering what I had done so wrong to be stuck in an apartment with such fake bastards. After drinking the bottle of wine I had brought alone, I left and hoped never to see any of these people ever again.

The summer continued on, and I was miserable. Nothing made me happy and everything bothered me. It was as if I had turned into a grumpy old man. Fearing I was going to turn into my grandfather, who in the last years of his life, sat on his front porch and yelled at the Japanese people who lived across the street from him, I tried to refocus my energy on moving back to New York. At this point, I had no ties to D.C., except my family, whom I could abandon at any moment and a serving job that I could not have cared less about. I arranged a few interviews in New York that summer but nothing panned out. The economy was taking a turn for the worse and the options for me were very limited everywhere. Fearing my livelihood was at stake, I asked Christopher, one of the owners of the café, if I could work for him part time. Christopher owned a small catering business that served healthy, organic food and were conscious to the earth and her many needs. All of the utensils they served food with were biodegradable and the cars they used to drive the food to the parties ran on electricity and used very little gas. The concept behind this business was amazing and I really wanted to be a part of the team. Christopher told me I could work for them on the weekdays as part of the street team. I was excited about my new vocation, the fourth this year, and eager to get away from the café and all of the drinking and debauchery that took place there.

I reported for my first day of duty and was excited about being part of the street team. When I got there, a friendly guy named Tom explained what I would be doing. He showed me around and told me that I would be taking one of the carts to the American History Museum and serving food there.

"Wait a second, I thought this was a catering company," I asked Tom.

"It is," he said, "But we also serve organic street food at the museums."

"So basically, I am a glorified hot dog vendor?" I asked.

"No, you are an organic food service distributor," Tom said.

"Are you serious?" I asked.

He was. Here we are in D.C., trying to be something we weren't, like everyone else. He went over the instructions of what I was supposed to do and where I was supposed to go. I still had no idea where I was half the time, so I told Tom that he was going to have to physically show me where I needed to be. I concluded that figuring my way around D.C. was pointless as I was trying to get out as soon as possible.

"You see Mark," Tom said, "D.C. is a grid, so if you just look at it like a grid, you will be fine."

"D.C. is not a grid. Grid's don't have circles and squares and roads that go diagonally."

"It's a grid," he said. "It's easy."

"No, Tom," I said, "New York is a grid. D.C. is a mess."

We fought about whether or not D.C. was in fact a grid for the next few minutes until Tom finally realized that I was right, as always. We went outside and Tom showed me how to use the cart that I would be driving to the museum. The cart ran on electricity so it did not go very fast, only about twenty-five miles an hour. It was also very delicate. The carts were designed specifically for this company and crafted with care, so they needed to be driven with caution. He went over a few more details and taught me how to serve the food and I was off to my first organic food distribution location.

"Don't kill anyone!" Tom yelled as I drove away. Those were my instructions every day thereafter.

I got in my cart and drove off the site. I am not a good driver to begin with. The cart was very fragile and every bump in the road I went over, felt like I had driven over a small canyon. It rattled and with every turn I just knew my cart was going to fall over on its side at any time. I thought I was going to crash several times as I drove down Pennsylvania Avenue towards the museums. I could not believe that my life had come to this. I was in still in D.C. and driving a fucking hot dog cart. How did this happen to me?

I got to the American History Museum and set up my cart. After I was done setting up, I ate about four hot dogs and waited for my first customers. I stood in my cart and all I could think of was how my parents stressed that if I did not go to college, I would never end up with a good job. Well, I had gone to college and now I was stuck in a cart selling food on the street. I guess had I not gone to college, I would have just ended up being a plain old hot dog vendor and not an organic food service distributor. As the seasons changed and it grew colder, my services were no longer needed with the hot dog carts. It was fine with me because during my tenure there, I ate more food than

I sold and nearly killed two people when I came dangerously close to hitting them with my cart.

By the time the 2008 general election rolled around, I had all but had it with politics. Everyone who came into the café talked about politics and I couldn't stand it anymore. My beloved Hillary Clinton had lost the primary vote and so I had lost all interest in the election. But everyone in D.C. was revved up for what was to be the party of the year. People in D.C. are so lame that any excuse to drink was a good one to them. They couldn't think of anything creative to do so they would use crappy excuses like Election Day and Bastille Day to get completely trashed. I could not have cared less about the election and made it known to anyone that would listen that I was writing Hillary Clinton's name on the ballot.

"Isn't that a waste of a vote?" a friend asked me.

"No," I said. "It is my duty as an American and I will vote for whomever I please. Please be assured, I am not voting for either one of those shmacockles."

"Whatever,"

I thought that Hillary deserved to be president. If nothing else the Clintons would bring a little class back to this shit hole of a town. But she was no longer a candidate and I watched with everyone else, as Barack Obama became the nation's forty-fourth president. Everyone went crazy in the streets of D.C. Yelling, looting and carrying about as if they were Jews that had just been freed from the concentration camps by the Americans. I didn't see what all of the fuss was about. I was tired of Washingtonians getting drunk all the time for no reason. Even I, the biggest drunk in the world, could not rationalize the reason people chose to drink. I just thought people were using lame excuses to drink to mask their own alcoholism. Washingtonians pretending to be something they weren't was becoming more unbearable by the minute. One night while waiting tables, Jim, the owner of the café came over to me and saw that I was upset. He asked me what the problem was and I told him that I hated D.C., everyone in it and was afraid that I was going to be stuck there for the rest of my life.

"Well, you're a writer. If you hate D.C. so much, why don't you just write a story about it?" he asked.

"Ok Jim," I said, "Let me write a story about how much I hate D.C. so everyone in this town can hate me even more than they already do. What a great idea."

MY SUPER EX-BOYFRIENDS

As far as I am concerned, relationships are for teenagers and immigrants. Apart from anyone not classified as one of the two, rarely have I seen a relationship work out. I guess there is something about being trapped in a math class or on a ship to the new world that makes the heart grow fonder. But I'll be damned if I didn't try. Throughout my clubbing, drugging and downright debauchery, I managed to find four real winners that stood apart from the rest. Sure, there were others along the way, but these four beaus were the cream of the crop, each one with a bizarre story to tell. The names of my former suitors have been changed to protect mainly, myself. For one thing had I not changed their names, I most likely would have been court ordered to and for another I really cannot afford to have the United States government and/or the armed forces up in my business.

My first boyfriend who I'll call Sebastian was a total gentleman. A British import, Sebastian had as much style as he had substance. Sebastian and I met through my former best friend Alex, who was dating Sebastian at the time. Sebastian and Alex's relationship was not a good one. Sebastian was twenty-eight years old and Alex was eighteen. Sebastian had a seventy-hour work week while Alex was a part-time drug dealer. Sebastian had responsibilities. Alex rolled on ecstasy about five times a week. Clearly this was not a match made in gay heaven, but Sebastian really cared for him. I guess he had a thing for eighteen-year-old Asian guys and really – who could blame him? At the center of this episode of *Gays of Our Lives* was yours truly. Because, as most dysfunctional relationships go, this one was weighed down by the fact that the three of us lived together. Sebastian and Alex had dated for about three months until Sebastian had finally had enough of Alex's antics. I was never really sure whether or not Alex really cared for Sebastian or if he was just taking advantage of his generosity, but I could tell that Sebastian was done.

When Sebastian finally decided to kick Alex out of the apartment, I had to side with Sebastian. For one thing, things were finally starting to come together for me. I had a great job and I was looking really good circa summer 2001. I was not really willing to put forth much effort into finding a new place to live. Secondly, while drug dealing is quite a lucrative vocation, Alex was beginning to sell drugs out of our apartment and the most unsavory people were beginning to hang around. Sebastian and I stood as a united front upon giving Alex the proverbial boot. While I was crushed by this decision, fearing for Alex's well being, I knew in the long run, it was most likely the best decision for us to make. Shortly after Alex left our apartment, Sebastian and I became very close. I had consoled him through his breakup and we had spent so much time together that suddenly I realized – I loved Sebastian. It was like at the end of *Clueless* when Alicia Silverstone suddenly realizes she loves her stepbrother. Except a lot less creepy. At the suggestion of my dear friend Jason, who may have been drunk at the time, Sebastian and I began dating. However, there were to be a few ground rules to be followed, but on my part only. According to Sebastian, I was never to speak to Alex again, which was a very harsh request considering Alex was my best friend at the time. At this point, Alex was going down a shadowy path, so I thought to detour myself from that it may be best for me to stop speaking to him. Something at that time told me this was the best decision to make, but I had no idea this one request from Sebastian was going to loom over the remainder of our relationship.

The summer of 2001 was magical. I had really captured the essence of being a functioning alcoholic. I partied hard but always managed to get my shit done. Sebastian and I spent all of our free time together and we were living it up. But the memory of Alex lingered. Both Sebastian and I still thought of Alex, respectively, and everything that happened between the three of us. One night mid-summer, I ended up bumping into Alex at one of our old haunts, Limelight. He was a complete mess but I walked over to say hello.

"Hey Alex," I shouted over the loud techno music.

"cdksjbfskgjhds," he replied.

"What?" I yelled. "Are you drunk?"

He didn't respond so I took that as a 'yes'. Shortly thereafter, Alex's friend gaily walked over and told me that both he and Alex were out of money and that they needed twenty dollars to get home. I felt awful after everything that happened between us so I gave him the money. I guess drug dealing wasn't the money making business I had once thought it was.

The next morning when I told Sebastian about this, he was furious. Mainly because I now needed twenty dollars from him to get to work.

"How could you give money to that little twit?" Sebastian barked in his British accent. Accents, by the way, are cute for the first few months of a relationship and then become extremely unbearable. The British think that they can get away with anything just by flashing their jacked up smile and offering you crisps or something. In American they are called chips. Potato chips! A nap is not a kip and a fag is most definitely not a cigarette. I tried to explain the situation to him but he was having none of it. For some reason, I apologized for giving Alex the money but Sebastian stewed over it for days. It was clear that Sebastian and I were having a great time, but Alex was certainly still pulling the strings.

That summer also happened to be when I had the absolute pleasure of meeting someone who would become a permanent fixture in my inner circle. His name was Tom and we met at a piano bar in the West Village when I told him to shut up while my friend Jason was singing. We took an immediate dislike to each other. However, after a few nights of drinking heavily and staying up for hours, we discovered that we both shared a passion for theatre, things that glittered and the 1980's primetime soap *Falcon Crest*. After only a week of bonding with my intellectual equal, Tom called with amazing news.

"I am going to Provincetown to do *Naked Boys Singing!*" he yelled into the phone.

I really only understood the naked boys part as I had no idea where Provincetown was or why exactly these boys would be singing naked. He explained he would be starring in an all nude, all male musical review on Cape Cod and I was thrilled for him. This was just the break in his career he was looking for, but it meant that he was going to be gone for the remainder of the summer.

"I'm leaving in a week and I need to lose thirty pounds," he said. "I can't be seen singing naked in this condition."

"What? You can't lose thirty pounds in a week. It's unhealthy," I said as I took a drag of my cigarette.

"Watch me!"

No one does a crash quite like Tom. He lost quite a few pounds before heading out of town. On his final night in New York, I helped him move things into a buddy's apartment in Queens. But on the subway ride over, I saw that he looked a little flushed. Luckily, I had a balance bar in my pocket.

"Eat this!" I said waving the balance bar in his face.

"Absolutely not," he replied. "I did not work this hard losing all of this weight to fuck it up now"

Fearing he was on the verge of death from malnutrition, I gave him the only other thing I had to offer: a bump of coke. Surprisingly, it helped, and I sent him on his way.

At the end of the summer, Tom and I decided to move in together. We thought that if I moved out of Sebastian's apartment it would not only be good for my relationship with Sebastian, but it would also free up a lot of time for Tom and I to get fucked up together. However, the apartment was not available until October 1st so I convinced Sebastian to let Tom stay at his place when he got back from Cape Cod until our apartment was ready. Tom returned on September 10th, 2001 looking tan, happy and anorexically thin. Apparently he had been hanging out with Karen Carpenter the whole time he was away. Nonetheless, it was great to have him back, and to celebrate we went out for a super classy dinner at Chevy's.

"Yea, I guess I am glad to be back," Tom said. "But I have a really ominous feeling that something bad is going to happen."

"Are you coming down off of something?" I asked.

"Maybe"

"That must be it."

That night we celebrated Tom's return and partied old school. The next morning, the world changed forever.

On the morning of September 11th...nay, the afternoon of September 11th, I woke to Tom yelling: "Hurry up Mark, you are going to miss *Falcon Crest!*"

Tom and I were very excited because that day SoapNet was playing the episode of *Falcon Crest* where Maggie tragically died in the swimming pool after getting her ring caught in the filter.

"I just don't understand why she didn't let the ring go," Tom asked.

"It's a pretty nice ring," I replied. "I would have fought for that shit too."

With such an intellectual conversation going on inside apartment 3H, it's no wonder Tom and I had no idea what was going on outside.

Sebastian entered and asked if either one of us wanted bagels from the deli downstairs. We put in our orders and I told Sebastian that if he was going to leave the house, he needed to put his contacts in. The man's blinder than a bat. Every time he left the apartment without them, I was scared he was going to get lost and traded into white slavery, never to return. But Sebastian left, sans contacts lenses and wandered onto University Place.

Apartment 3H backed up to a brick wall. While it was not the most scenic of views, it made for great sleeping conditions. It was pitch black at all hours of the day and you could never hear what was going on outside. It was perfect for hangovers.

While Tom and I sat discussing whether or not *Falcon Crest* was, in fact, the best show ever, I had completely forgotten that I was supposed to meet my friend Michele for lunch.

I grabbed my phone to call her, but it went straight to voicemail: "Michele, you dumb bitch, where are you? We were supposed to have lunch but I can't make it down to Wall Street today. I have to work in Times Square at three and it's already 12:30, and I have to watch the end of *Falcon Crest* so let's reschedule. Love you, bye." As I hung up the phone, Sebastian came back into the apartment in a panic.

"What's up honey?" I asked.

"Nothing. I went to the deli and people were going crazy outside," he said, "There must have been a school trip or something going on because people were buying water bottles by the dozens and everyone seemed in a bigger rush than usual."

"That's odd," I responded. "Where's my bagel?"

We sat and ate our bagels. Maggie died in the pool. I got ready for work and Sebastian got ready for a job interview. I am pretty sure that Tom had planned on staying in and watching soap operas from the 80's all day. *Knots Landing* was about to come on when my phone rang for the first time that day.

I answered. "What the fuck is wrong with you?" my mother yelled into the phone.

"Uh. Nothing. Why?" I replied.

"You stupid son of bitch. Why haven't you called me?"

"I was watching *Falcon Crest*. Was I supposed to call you?"

"You have got to be fucking kidding me!" my mother yelled. "Do you have any idea what the fuck is going on around your dumb ass?"

"Well, Maggie just died in the pool if that's what you were talking about"

"Jesus! The city of New York is under attack. The World Trade Center is gone and I have been trying to call you for hours now. I have been so worried, but I should have known that your dumb gay ass would be sitting around watching crappy soaps from the 80's."

"*Falcon Crest* is a great show!"

"Well, I am glad you're not dead." Click. She hung up. At 1:15 in the afternoon of September 11th, 2001, Sebastian, Tom and I finally realized what was going on around us. SoapNet had not pre-empted programming so we didn't see the news because we hadn't changed the channel. Everyone at the deli was getting bottled water because pandemonium was ensuing around them. Sebastian had not noticed that two huge towers, the largest in New York, were missing form the skyline because he didn't put his contacts in before leaving the apartment.

It took us a couple of minutes to realize what was happening. Michele called that night and yelled at me for calling her a dumb bitch. She didn't pick up her phone when I called because she was running for her life across the Brooklyn Bridge. That night Tom fled to Queens to stay with friends, fearing the terrorists were going to find him if he stayed in Manhattan. He later became the self proclaimed Queen of Queens. Sebastian and I stayed in Apartment 3H, glued to the television and began the final weeks of our relationship.

After September 11th, Tom and I decided to support the economy of New York by going out and drinking as much as humanly possible. On one particular night we got really trashed and I ended up kissing some random guy. It was then I realized that I loved Sebastian.

"You know Tom, doing that, going out on a limb like that, really made me realize how much I really really love Sebastian," I slurred, clutching my drink as if my life depended on it.

"Uh, yea. Kissing a stranger will do that," Tom replied.

Tom and I drunkenly swaggered back to the apartment around three o'clock in the morning and I decided that then was the perfect time to tell Sebastian that I loved him. I woke him up from a sound sleep.

"I love you. I am in love with you!" I screamed into his face, my breath smelling of forty-five vodka cocktails.

"You're drunk," Sebastian replied. Not really the response I was going for.

"Yes. But, I am telling you that I love you."

There was a very long, very uncomfortable pause. Tom was drunkenly swaying there, watching this train wreck take place.

"I SAID I LOVE YOU!" I shouted.

And finally, after what felt like an hour, Sebastian replied: "That's nice. Thank you."

I passed out. The next morning, I woke up feeling as if I chartered a flight to the Dewar's plant the night before and drank everything inside.

"Do you remember what you did last night?" Tom asked.

"Uh, kind of," I replied. After Tom so graciously filled me in, I asked him what I should do next.

"I don't know," he responded, "See how things go after we move into *Falcon Crest*." We had decided that our new apartment was going to be named *Falcon Crest* – it seemed only fitting. "You guys have been spending far too much time together. Perhaps, after you move out he will realize what his real feelings for you are."

Maybe not – I thought. Deep down inside I knew moving was not going to help, but I decided to see how things went.

October 1st finally came and Tom and I moved into *Falcon Crest*. To celebrate moving into our new digs, we decided to throw an "opening night" party. Cheap five-dollar bottles of vodka were poured into crystal decanters and huge bags of Doritos were put into tin bowls. It was to be a gala event. However, that evening, Sebastian called and told me that he had gone to a party the night before, where Alex was in attendance. He said that he wanted to see him for one reason or another. I was floored. I had only moved out of his apartment days before and he was already going to parties where he knew Alex was going to be. I was told at the beginning of the summer that Alex was bad and I was to steer clear of him. Now Sebastian was going out of his way to see Alex. Were we still dating? Was Sebastian simply waiting for me to leave the apartment to start another fling with Alex? I was crushed but I knew what I had to do. I broke up with Sebastian – took one of the crystal decanters filled with five-dollar vodka and retreated to my room, where I stayed for the next three days. I completely missed the *Falcon Crest* opening night party and sat for three days watching *Beaches* on rotation while drinking vodka. I was devastated by what happened – I felt my love life was spiraling out of control. Finally, Tom intervened.

"Look, you have been drinking by yourself for the past three days," Tom said. "Remember when Maggie turned into a raging alcoholic on *Falcon Crest*? Did we not learn a lesson? When you drink by yourself for days at a time you are an alcoholic. So get your ass up and get some drinks with me. At least you won't be drinking alone."

Tom's persuasion worked. I figured going out would help me take my mind off of Sebastian, but when we got out, who was the first person we ran into? Why Alex, of course.

I was about as excited to see him, as I was when I found out that Paris Hilton was putting an album out. By this point, Alex had turned into a full on arch nemesis. He was the Alexis to my Krystal Carrington. Things were being said about me behind my back that I really did not appreciate and Sebastian had done a great job of pitting the two of us against each other.

"I don't like him," Tom said as Alex sashayed his way toward us.

"Thanks, but you don't even know him," I replied.

"I've known people who have looked like him before and I didn't like them so I don't like him."

Alex came over and began running his mouth about how I was getting what I deserved because I had betrayed him. I was already drunk from my three-day rendezvous in my room and I could not listen to much of Alex's babbling. I began to walk away when Alex mentioned that he was planning on meeting up with Sebastian the following night. I was furious. Had there been a lily pond near by, I would have thrown his ass right into it. I gave Alex a dirty look and walked right out the door. I walked down Sixth Avenue, fuming, and wondering what the hell Sebastian was thinking. He told me that I needed to cut off all communication with Alex. I had stupidly assumed that the same rules had applied for Sebastian but they hadn't. I could not believe the hypocrisy of it all. Sebastian's excuse for everything was that he had real feelings for Alex and my friendship was a constant reminder of those feelings. Now it seemed I was the only one looking out for my feelings. As all of these thoughts raced through my head, I raced down the avenue to Sebastian's.

Out of breath from chain smoking during the walk, I arrived at Sebastian's. He opened the door.

"Bugger! What are you doing here?" There was the damned accent again.

"Shut up – I'm coming in," I said as I made my way toward the wet bar. I poured myself a huge glass of vodka – my drink of choice for the past three odd days – and parked myself on his couch. "Why on earth would you be asking Alex out again?"

"I suppose you've seen him?" he responded.

"No dumbass. I've acquired psychic abilities in the four days that we haven't been dating. Of course I saw him and he could not wait to tell me the news," I yelled, with my glass of vodka swishing this way and that. "Honestly, I cannot believe that you are doing this. Do you even have feelings for him?"

"I don't think so," he said, meekly. "But, I wanted to make sure."

"Excuse me? You don't *think* so? What the hell is that supposed to mean?"

"I am not sure. I am just very confused about my feelings right now."

I was really not in the mood for this. I had consumed about a year and a half's supply of vodka over the previous three days and Sebastian's indecisiveness was grating on my nerves. I really didn't feel like going around in circles anymore. I needed at least twenty-four hours of sleep and possibly a trip to a rehab clinic.

"Ok fine," I got up. "Well…ok then," I said stumbling toward the door. I could not think of anything else to say so I told him to call Alex and tell him that they were not going to be able to get together the next night because we were back together.

"What?" Sebastian asked.

"We are back together," I told him. "I just decided. Tell Alex we are back together. I am only looking out for you. Do you really want to get involved with someone like that again? Remember how miserable you were? So really, I am doing you a favor. I am saving you from yourself." If only I could have taken my own advice and saved myself but it was too late. On the way out I took the glass I was drinking out of and threw it at the wall. Mostly for dramatic effect, but also to show him that I meant business. The next day we were back together and Alex seemed to be out of the picture. Tom, however, was not happy about any of my recent behavior and told me that he thought I was not making the best decisions for myself.

"I think it's time that you put this booze cruise in dry dock for a bit," he said.

It was true. I wasn't making good decisions anymore. For another couple of months, Sebastian and I continued to date, but it wasn't the same and we finally broke up for good.

Again, I was not very happy about this decision. Sebastian was my first boyfriend and I could honestly not imagine my life without him. Pair that with the fact that the two of us continued to sleep with each other for the year and half after we broke up – things were not looking good for my sanity.

Finally, I dropped my basket. Through some computer sleuthing (I guessed the password for Sebastian's email account. It was Paddington Bear. Easy for me to decode as it was his favorite story when he was a child. And he's British – how difficult could it have been? Maybe he wasn't as smart as I thought he was.) I discovered that Sebastian had yet again been corresponding with Alex. If my life was a soap opera, this storyline had been going on for far too long at this point. No one wanted to hear about it anymore. There needed to be a dramatic ending, climaxing with the ingénue (me) coming out triumphant and relatively unscathed.

For months I had threatened to tell Sebastian ubber-conservative parents that he was gay. I knew it was an awful thing to do, but at this point, I had no other choice. What would Erica Kane have done? I was too young for a hostile takeover and I really don't think I could have pulled off an insanity plea in a murder case just yet so this seemed to be the next logical step. La Kane would have also tried to sleep with someone else to make her former suitor jealous, but since Sebastian had already encouraged me to do that, it clearly would not work at getting him back. I even tried a half-assed, very dramatic suicide attempt but that didn't even work. So I did it. I sent his parents a very long and very detailed letter, with pictures, via first class mail. I, of course, had to call Sebastian and tell him that I was sending it and that was the last time we ever spoke. I was so hurt by everything that had happened between the two of us, I felt like I needed to make him pay for hurting my feelings; however, it didn't make me feel any better. In fact, it made me feel awful. I did truly love Sebastian and did not want to hurt him, but this back and forth between us had to end. I will always hold a special place in my heart for Sebastian. He was and still is an amazing person, and my time with him was the best of my life.

A few years after I sent the letter to his parents, I bumped into Sebastian and his new boyfriend Jesse. Sebastian and I became very good friends and all was seemingly forgiven. That is of course, until he reads this.

It took me some time to get over Sebastian and realize what I had done was possibly the worst thing anyone had ever done to him. But being the self-proclaimed survivor that I am, I trudged on. A few years later, Tom was in a full-fledged relationship with his now husband Michael while he was performing in his own Off-Broadway hit musical. His show opened to much acclaim and seeing Tom entertain anyone other than me is always a treat. The show went on every Sunday night and afterwards we would go down to the West Village to a piano bar where our friend Kate worked. One Sunday night, my friend Jason (previously responsible for suggesting Sebastian and I date), met us at the bar with his boyfriend Mark. By this point my drinking had plateaued and I was at a very happy place with it. I had stopped getting hammered every night, instead enjoying just a drink or two. Seeing my two best friends happy was amazing. Tom was with Michael and enjoying the success of a very popular Off-Broadway show; while Jason was paired with Mark who was musically directing a very popular Broadway show at the time. Everyone was happily paired and working in the theatre. It was like everyone was living the gay-dream. Had Liza Minnelli been lowered down from the ceiling on a disco ball that night, everyone's lives would have been complete. I, on the other hand, was living my life vicariously through Tom and Jason and had absolutely no problem being single. But, it seemed everyone else has a problem with it. I was constantly being invited to parties where someone's single gay friend was going to be only to find that their single gay friend was either over fifty, had at one point been in a mental institution, or just completely incapable of carrying on an intelligent conversation. I mean, I love Madonna as much as the next guy, but there is only so much I want to know about her life. ABC soaps on the other hand, I could talk about for hours. Needless to say everyone had pretty much given up on paring me off until Jason's boyfriend Mark introduced me to his friend Jeff that fateful night. Jeff seemed perfect on paper. Tall, dark and handsome – just the way I liked them. He had worked with Mark in Chicago (the city, not the musical), the previous year, musically directing a show out there. Jeff came highly recommended from Mark and Jason and I could see why. Maybe this was my second chance. Maybe my karma wasn't completely fucked for what I had done to Sebastian. Jeff and I ended up closing the bar that night. We were so busy talking and getting to know each other; I guess time just got away from us. As Jason was leaving, he came over to me and whispered in my ear: "Don't do anything I wouldn't do."

"Ok, Jason," I said. "That would pretty much just rule out women and midgets, so I think I will be just fine."

Jason could obviously see where this was going. After he left, Jeff and I continued drinking and I guess I had about three too many cocktails when he asked me to come home with him. I told him that I had a very strict policy on going home with guys. That was, I would not go home with a guy if I had to walk up more than five flights of stairs to get to his apartment. He told me he lived in a sixth floor walk-up. It was settled, he would have to come to mine.

We hooked up that night and it was amazing. The next day, I had class so I had to run off. That evening he called me to tell me that he was by my apartment and the sun was setting over the Hudson River and he wanted to see it with me. This was only day two, granted, but so far so good. Besides, the holidays were coming up and it's always nice to have a beau around Christmastime. I had my eyes on a pair of Louis Vutton rain boots, but figured it was way too early to stop dropping hints. Things with Jeff were great for about a week. We cooked dinner for each other, hung out all of the time and really enjoyed each other's company. But once week two rolled around, Jeff began asking questions that made me start thinking that something was up.

One night after we had sex he asked me: "What's the absolute worst thing that you have ever done?"

I had to think about this one. Telling Jeff about outing Sebastian to his parents was a little too dramatic a tale for week two of a relationship.

"Ummm...I don't know. I once stole a sweater from a department store." Which was a total lie; unless by saying once I meant twenty-five thousand times. I had a brief addiction with stealing things that weren't mine a few years beforehand, but it had passed, and again these fun facts about my past were better saved for a conversation in year two or three of a relationship.

"Oh," Jeff sighed as he grimaced. Was he expecting me to say that I had murdered someone at one point? Did this guy get off on these sorts of things?

"What's the worst thing you've ever done?" I asked.

He told me that he couldn't tell me. I became scared. Was this seemingly nice pianist a serial killer? Fearing I may be murdered in my sleep, I told Jeff that I had a paper I needed to finish and that he had to leave. Shit! It was only day nine of the relationship and I was already suspicious that my new lover muffin was a psycho killer who wore his prays skins over his own after he killed them. I, of course, must jump to the most ridiculous of conclusions. Later that night, Jeff called to explain.

"Sorry I was so weird before," he said as I listened on the phone. I think I was only half paying attention to him because there was a really good rerun of *Melrose Place* on but here is what I remember:

"I asked you what the worst thing you had ever done was because I have done something bad in my past. One night a few years ago, when my ex and I were living together, a fire started in the apartment below us. It was awful – we could not get through our door so we had to climb out of our window and down the fire escape. On our way down, we saw that our downstairs neighbor, who was an older woman, was trapped in her apartment. My boyfriend went down to the street to call for help while I tried to help our neighbor out of her apartment. I tried to help her but couldn't and told her to stay and wait until the fire fighters got there. But help came too late and she ended up dying in her apartment. I couldn't help her and I have felt awful ever since."

Now I felt awful. What a hero Jeff was. What a shame he couldn't help that woman. How terrible he must have felt to feel so powerless. Now I felt like a complete asshole. Not only had I stolen thousands of dollars worth of merchandise from department stores all over the New York metro area, I was also too lazy to walk up the six flights of stairs to Jeff's apartment, let alone try and help a 150-pound geriatric out of a burning building.

"That is nothing to be ashamed of," I said. "You did the best you could have done, but you couldn't have prevented the inevitable." At this point in the conversation, my Tylenol PM was kicking in so I had to get off of the phone. I said goodnight and hung up.

"There has to be more to the story than that!" Tom said the next afternoon over a plate of scrambled eggs. On days when I did not have classes in the afternoon, Tom and I would meet up for lunch and roam the city discussing important topics such as the goings on of the ABC soaps and whatever happened to the careers of people like Bonnie Franklin from *One Day at A Time*.

"I really don't think so Tom," I said as I gracefully scarffed down a tuna melt. "He seemed to be on the verge of tears when he was explaining what happened. I really think he is fairly heroic."

"I don't know," Tom replied. "I don't have a good feeling about this one."

I stopped eating. Tom had suspicions about Jeff. This was not good. This son of a bitch had practically predicted Sept. 11 and Gillian's untimely demise on *All My Children*. If Tom had a bad feeling about something, it was usually not a good sign.

"But it's almost the holidays! I could really use a boyfriend right now."

"I'm just telling you, I have a bad feeling about this guy. You know I am always right about these things."

Damn it! I knew Tom had to have been right and that there had to be more to this story than what Jeff was telling me. But, before I cut him off completely, I decided to do some more digging. I called Jeff and he asked me if I wanted to come over for dinner – I accepted.

When I got to Jeff's apartment, it looked beautiful. There were candles lit and a fabulous looking dinner had been made. I had just scored some weed and in my usual fashion of keeping things classy, I asked

Jeff if he wanted to smoke.

"Uh, no thanks. I can't," he replied.

"Oh no. Anyone can. I'll show you how to," I said as I began to roll a joint and begin a pantomime demonstration of how to smoke a j.

"No Mark, I know how to smoke. I just can't. I have court ordered drug tests once a week."

Fucking Tom was right again. I mean normal people do not spend their Friday mornings peeing into a cup in front of an officer of the court. I was really beginning to get worried now.

"Care to elaborate?" I asked as kindly as possible as I poured two thirds of a bottle of red wine into a 7-11 Big Gulp cup.

"Well I was going to tell you the second part of the story," he said. I knew there had to be more to Jeff's heroic adventures than he was letting on. Perhaps he accidentally set the fire, which would have been totally understandable. Or he was a pyromaniac, which was definitely not acceptable.

"I told you about the fire," he said as if I had completely blocked out the previous nights conversation. I gave him the *yeah-dumbass-you-did* look and he continued: "Well after the fire, my boyfriend and I moved downtown but things had changed. Shortly after we moved, we ended up breaking up and I was beginning to become afraid of sleeping at night because that's when the fire had started. Anyway, someone told me that if I took crystal meth, I could stay up all night and sleep some during the day." I really didn't like where this was going, "I was all alone after my boyfriend left me and I started doing crystal all the time. Then one night, a few months ago, I was on a date and the police came into my apartment. They confiscated all of my computers and drugs and had me arrested."

I thought there had to be a huge part of this story missing.

"Were you selling drugs?" I asked.

"No."

"What the hell were you doing then? Why did the police take your computers?"

"Well, apparently I downloaded some child pornography while I was high on crystal."

I guess I wasn't taking this one home to meet the parents.

"Ummm…ok," I murmured. I sat there, staring at his face and all I saw was one huge red flag.

"I didn't mean to," he said.

"Well there is a huge difference between someone who is ten and someone who is twenty, so please explain to me how you *didn't mean to.*"

"I was high."

If I had not used that excuse so many times in the past, it wouldn't have worked. And considering I still had half a glass of wine left and it would take me a good ten minutes to get down the stairs of his apartment, I decided I would let him explain.

"When I was high on crystal, I didn't know what I was doing half the time. I don't really like child pornography, but I just didn't know better."

Don't really like? That's not really the excuse I was looking for. I chugged my glass of wine and left.

"You're dating kiddie porn!" Tom shouted the next day at lunch.

"Not funny," I replied.

"Ha, ha, ha. I told you so!"

"Yeah, I know. I just feel really bad."

"Why?" Tom asked, looking confused.

"I don't know. I guess with the fire and everything. It's just a shame."

"It's disgusting is what it is," Tom replied, "And the fact that you look sixteen years old yourself isn't a really good defense for his case."

At that point I did look like I was sixteen years old. By age twenty-two, I really didn't look like I could have been out of high school. I guess I have really good genes. But years of excessive tanning and heavy drinking have since changed things.

"I guess I really can't date him anymore, huh?" I asked.

"No shit!" Tom replied. "And what the hell were Jason and Mark doing setting you up with this guy anyway?"

"That's a great question."

The next day, I met Jason and Mark for drinks and filled them in on what Jeff had told me.

"What the fuck were you two doing setting me up with kiddie porn?" I asked drunkenly.

"I didn't know any of this," Jason replied.

"Well, when we were working in Chicago, he was kind of up all night every night if I recall. I thought he may have had a drug problem, but didn't think it was that bad," Mark said.

"What the fuck makes you think that would make a good candidate for a boyfriend?" I asked.

"I don't know. It had kind of been a while," Mark replied.

Apparently, I was desperate enough, in my friend's eyes to date a drug-addicted pedophile. I left Mark and Jason and reminded myself never to let friends set me up with anyone ever again. Jeff called later that evening and I told him that I was not going to be able to see him anymore, for the obvious reasons. He told me that he understood and that it was all right because he was seeing someone else anyway.

Excuse me? When did twenty-eight year old, crystal meth smoking, child pornography enthusiasts become a hot commodity? My secretary must have forgotten to drop that memo on my desk. The "kiddie porn" debacle left me even more jaded than ever before. A few months later, I heard that Jeff did in fact go to jail and was there for a year and a half. A few years later, I was enjoying a lovely lunch by myself, reading a newspaper (aka Soap Opera Digest), when a gay couple sat down next to me. I eavesdropped on their conversation for a bit and then put my newspaper down only to find the gay couple was Jeff and his boyfriend who looked like he as about thirteen years old. It's nice to know that the justice system does in fact work and that some things will never change.

There is nothing – I mean nothing – I love more than a good old-fashioned night of binge drinking, and that's exactly what Jason and I did the night he and his significant other, Mark, broke up.

"Good riddance!" I said. "He set me up with kiddie porn. That's reason enough to break up with him." Jason and I were finally single together, for the first time in years. "Mothers, lock up your daughters! Mark and Jason are painting the town drunk tonight!"

And that's exactly what we did on the first night of Jason's freedom. We went to all of our favorite haunts and had an absolute blast. I wanted Jason to know that being single was just as much fun, if not more so, than having a boyfriend and I proved it by getting him and myself blackout drunk.

The next morning, I woke up severely hung-over. Like wanting to die hung-over. Except, I was not alone.

"Hey," the man in my bed said.

I must have had a gimlet or twelve too many the night before. I had to get this stranger out of room before anyone saw him and pronto.

"Uh, hi," I said with a half smile. "What a night last night, huh?"

"You have no idea who I am do you?" the man asked.

"Not a clue."

"I have the same name as your brother," he said.

"Tony?"

"No. Kevin." Damn my mother for having that third son. "Don't worry. We didn't do anything last night. We got home and you passed out."

What a refreshing thought. What a gentleman for not taking advantage of me or killing me in my sleep. That thought quickly passed as I had apparently drank quicksand the night before and needed some serious libations. I grabbed the jumbo-sized water bottle that was next to my bed and put it to my lips.

"Don't drink that!" Kevin shouted, as he grabbed the water bottle from my hand. "I couldn't find the bathroom last night so I peed into your water bottle."

A gentlemen indeed. At least he was keeping things classy. I felt bad for wanting to kick him out of my apartment so abruptly, so we sat on my bed and chatted for hours. Apparently, Kevin had the same love for ABC soaps that I did. This was huge because, as many know, soap operas have been a pivotal part of my life since age five and anyone who loves ABC soaps as much as I do was good people in my book.

"What about *Loving?*" I asked, wondering if he had the same affection for the now defunct soap as I did.

He smiled with glee: "Oh my God, I *loved Loving*! I was so sad when it was cancelled and they moved to *The City*. I mean I love Morgan Fairchild as much as the next guy, but things just weren't the same. Remember when Jeremy died in the poisonous plaster of Paris? That was TV at its finest."

I thought I could have been in love. We sat in bed for hours talking about soaps, Britney Spears and other important aspects of life. We then decided to grab some lunch at the café across the street from my apartment. I discovered that Kevin and I had a lot more in common than just soap operas. Pair that with the fact that he was quite a looker; things seemed to be going well for me that day. Kevin was half Irish and half Cuban, a combination that proved to be a good one. We ate and chatted and he told me that he had to go to a birthday party that evening and I could join him if I wanted. I told him I would be happy to go. He stated that he needed to go back to his apartment to change and we would meet up later at my place. We parted ways and I felt like I was floating on a cloud. The previous night I had gone out to celebrate being single but maybe being single wasn't all that great. Maybe having a boyfriend was the way to go after all. Besides, it was the boring part of the year between New Year's and spring and it would keep me busy if nothing else.

I was so excited about my potential boyfriend that I had to call someone. I picked up my cell and called my best gal pal Evelyn.

"Hey girl. What's going on?" I asked.

"Oh, nothing. Natalie and I just went to see the CHRONICles of Narnia. Ha, ha, ha," she replied.

"You dumbass. Evelyn, I have to tell you, I just met the most wonderful guy! He just turned up in my bed this morning."

"I love it when that happens," she replied.

"I know, right?" As I opened the door to my apartment, I gasped. I had not lived there for very long but since we were on the first floor, I figured that we would eventually have mice. But nothing could prepare me for what I saw in the kitchen.

"Evelyn, I gotta go!" I hung up the phone.

I put my keys down and walked into the kitchen. It was beginning to get cold outside, so the week before I had put out mice traps because I knew when the weather changed, the mice would naturally want to come in from the cold. But nothing, in my twenty-three years prepared me for this.

I had wisely decided to use glue traps to kill the mice because I thought it would make for a clean death. I didn't realize how wrong I was. I peered over the trashcan and found that at least two-dozen mice had fought an all out war where no one emerged the victor. My kitchen had turned into a virtual battlefield of mice. Some had lost limbs after trying to escape the glue traps and others had been eaten half to death. It was the most disgusting sight I had ever seen. After throwing up in my mouth, I decided I would have to clean the mess up myself. Both of my roommates were gone for the weekend and God forbid Kevin see the massacre that had taken place in my kitchen. In order to clean up, I needed some liquid courage. Besides, alcohol kills germs and that was reason enough for me to start drinking. I opened the freezer to grab a bottle of vodka and saw that there was a shoebox next to it. I opened the shoebox and found three more dead mice. I ran from the kitchen and called my roommate Catlin. Yes, Catlin. Not Caitlin. I told her when I moved in that I thought she had a bullshit name and that I would be referring to her as Jane from then on.

"Jane!" I yelled into the phone.

"Greetings from Cabo!" she answered.

"Why the hell are there three dead mice in our freezer?" I could tell that she was clearly having a good time and that I was clearly ruining it.

"Oh that," she said nonchalantly. "I found three mice in the glue traps and I totally freaked out so I ran upstairs and asked that crazy old lady what I should do. She told me that if I put them in the freezer they would die peacefully."

"Well, thanks for the heads up."

"Yeah, it was like right before I left for Cabo," she said

"Jane, you left for Cabo a week ago."

"Well, I meant to tell you, but I guess I forgot." She was drifting away from the conversation. "Oh, Margaritas! I'll have one."

"Thanks Jane, for nothing!"

"Mark, how many times do I have to tell you that my name is not Jane it's –."

I hung up on her. This is what you get for living with girls. I left the kitchen, put on some sweats, a do rag and huge yellow rubber gloves. I took the bottle of vodka in one hand and got down on my hands and knees and started scrubbing my kitchen floor, which looked liked a crime scene. I had little time to clean before Kevin got back so when scrubbing was not working, I dumped a bottle of bleach on the floor and began mopping. After a while, the vodka and fumes of the cleaning products had gotten to me, and I ended up passing out in bed for a while. I woke up, do rag and sweat pants still in tact to Kevin calling, telling me that he was at my door ringing the buzzer. Shit! I looked like crap and my whole apartment smelled like a community swimming pool. I got up and answered the door. I was so embarrassed. I told him that *Saving Private Ryan* had taken place in my kitchen except no one had been saved because all of the mice were dead. After all of the bleach that had been poured on my kitchen floor, there was still a smattering of blood. I had no choice but to tell him the truth because it looked like someone had delivered a dumpster prom baby in my kitchen. He laughed, he thought it was funny and told me that if I had waited, he would have helped me clean up. I told him how nice I thought he was because if I showed up at his apartment and there were thirty dead mice on his kitchen floor, I would have gone to the bar downstairs and told him to call me when he was done cleaning up.

We had a few laughs and he told me that we needed to head over to his friend Kate's apartment. I was in no state for a party. I would have to shower for at least forty-five minutes to cleanse myself of the day's events and I was starting to feel sick from the bleach and the three glasses of straight vodka I had downed that afternoon. Kevin reached into his bag, pulled out a black can and told me if I drank it I would feel better. The label on the can read SPARKS, but I had no idea what it was.

"What the hell is this?" I asked.

"You've never had Sparks?" he replied, surprised.

"No."

"It's like caffeinated beer."

"So do you drink this in lieu of coffee in the morning or is this just a pick me up?"

"It's just a pick me up!"

I just wanted to clear that up before I started inadvertently drinking beer for breakfast. And so a brief love affair with Sparks began. I drank it while I took an hour-long shower and came out feeling refreshed, nearly forgetting the scene from *Saving Private Ryan* that had taken place in my apartment just hours before.

Kevin and I went to Kate's party and had a blast. She lived in an art deco building in the west twenties and all of their friends were super fun. We all had a blast and drank and laughed all night long. If we kept this up we were sure to be New York's favorite party couple by months end. After the party, we went back to my apartment. As we walked in, I checked the kitchen to make sure that *Saving Private Ryan II: Ryan's Revenge* hadn't taken place in my kitchen. It hadn't and we went back to my room and started making out like teenagers. I suddenly realized that in all of the commotion of the day, Kevin and I still hadn't hooked up. He was a really good kisser and I could sense that things were moving in the right direction. After about a half hour of making out, I decided to take things to the next level. I stuck my hands down his pants and felt around. At first, I found nothing, but after a few seconds, I wrapped my finger around one of the most offensively small penises I had ever felt. It was a good thing it was dark or else Kevin would have seen the utter confusion on my face. He was a good four inches taller than me – surely this must have been some sort of glitch. I took his pants off and started rubbing it – but nothing happened. That's as big as it was going to get. I had about the same level of excitement going into this hook up as I did when my brother got a big screen TV for Hanukah and I got a poster. Being resilient, I did the job using the tools I had to the best of my abilities. It was painstaking, but when someone presents a job that may not be the best offer you've ever received, I was always told to take it.

"That was awesome!" he cried out after I finished the job.

"Uh, yeah." I said. I lay down next to him. I figured I could not tell this guy that my six-month old nephew's penis was potentially bigger than his, after a day that involved an entire bottle of vodka and a rodent genocide in my own home, I was too tired to bring it up.

Hung-over again! I thought as I woke up the next morning. However, instead of being able to sleep it off, I had to go into the office. At that point, I was working at a very prestigious advertising agency. Having rolled in more than once hung-over, I was beginning to think that the higher-ups thought that I had a drinking problem. I jumped into the shower and put on my suit but still felt like death.

"I feel like shit," I told Kevin. "I don't know how I am going to get through the day." Kevin reached into his pocket and pulled out a pill. "What the hell is that?"

"It's a xanex," he said. "It's fabulous for hangovers."

I hadn't planned on starting a pill addiction until my mid-40's, but he said it worked wonders, and at the point I would have taken anything to stop my ears from ringing.

I got to the office and immediately went to my friend Anna's cube. Anna and I became fast friends at the agency. We shared a mutual hatred for just about everyone and she smoked almost as much as I did so it was love at first sight. I filled her in on the weekend's events.

"That sucks about the mice," Anna said pretending to do her job. Apparently, this was the most entertaining part of the story for her. She stopped typing and looked at me, "As far as the guy goes, sure he has a small penis. All Irish guys do." While Anna was studying at Notre Dame, she conducted a little survey with her friends to see what ethnicity had the largest and smallest penises. "That was a great semester," Anna continued, "We concluded that the Irish have the smallest penises after combining our research."

"I wish you had told me this before I had to go down on my own pinky finger."

"You didn't call," she replied.

"Oh well, I really like him anyway."

"That's great!" she smiled.

"What did you do this weekend?" I asked.

"I found out that my stupid fucking husband got me pregnant about a month ago," There goes another smoking buddy.

The week ended up going by quickly. I didn't get a chance to see Kevin but we had made plans to go to dinner that Thursday. Small penis aside, he was a really nice guy and I loved hanging out with him. That week, my friend Chad from Atlanta was coming into town on business and drunken shenanigans were sure to ensue. Chad was always fun to be around and one of the hottest guys I had ever laid my eyes on. The summer before, when Chad had come to visit, I became borderline obsessed with him. He didn't return the interest so I just let it be, but enjoyed his company nonetheless. When I told Kevin that one of the hottest guys in the world was coming to visit, Kevin insisted that we make things exclusive between us. I am sure telling Kevin that Chad was hot was not something he really wanted to hear, but what can I say? He's *really* hot and I calls 'em like I sees 'em.

Could I deal with Kevin's abnormally small penis forever? I didn't know if I wanted exclusivity but figured Cher stayed with Sonny for a long time and he was just taller than a dwarf. I decided to be exclusive with Kevin and put dreams of bigger penises on the back burner. Thursday had rolled around and instead of going out to dinner we ended up drinking absurd amounts of vodka and ordering pizza. Could this guy be the one? It doesn't take much to impress me and he was definitely on his way to Loverville.

Within the next few days, it was time for the ritual unveiling of the new boyfriend to Tom. We all met for drinks at our favorite piano bar. Kevin and I had not drank much that evening, something I made sure of. If Tom had told me that he didn't like this one, I knew he would need to be dumped. He was always right about these things and I knew that Kevin would need to be on his best behavior in order to not jinx it.

Everything seemed to go off without a hitch. Tom brought his boyfriend Michael and his friend Cindy. We had a few drinks and a few laughs while watching the performers sing. After going our separate ways, Kevin and I returned to his apartment, which we had basically turned into a frat house. I guess it was more like a gay frat house because there was a lot of homosexual kissing going on, not something you normally see on university campuses. Making out with Kevin always led to heavy petting. More on his part than mine, I'm afraid. I was secretly hoping that his penis had miraculously grown over night, but much to my chagrin, when I pulled down his pants, there was his little half-incher. I was just drunk enough to go for it. I was not going to let this, or any other little penis get in the way of my happiness. Besides, Valentine's Day was right around the corner and I told myself that I was not going to spend another Valentine's Day getting drunk by myself and watching *Steel Magnolias*. I flipped him over. I meant business. As I began to move the sex train in the direction I thought it needed to be going, Kevin began wailing like a child.

"What's wrong with you? I haven't even done anything yet!" I said trying to console him.

"I was molested at summer camp when I was thirteen," he cried.

This was not the time, nor the place to have this conversation, but I rolled over, pulled the covers up and patted his head. If conservatives ever wanted to make a commercial about why gay sex is bad – they should have come in with a camera crew at that moment. I leaned over to listen to Kevin's story. He told me that a camp counselor had touched him inappropriately when he was a teenager. I guess I didn't understand because I would have probably not only encouraged that kind of behavior, but it most likely would have saved a lot of awkward moments for me in high school. I listened to his story and as he finished he said:

"Thanks for listening and understanding. I love you."

Wait…what? I had known this guy for two weeks and he was already dropping *L bombs*. No one had ever told me that they loved me before and the only time I had ever said it to anyone was to Sebastian after a night that should have landed me in rehab. So I replied: "I love you too?" What was I supposed to do? He was crying hysterically for over an hour and I didn't want to hurt his feelings any more. We went to bed that night and we never spoke of that incident again. I guess he didn't want anyone to know…woops.

Kevin's confession was not the only thing that led to the demise of our relationship. He only wanted to see me on certain nights of the week – never on Mondays, Wednesdays or Thursdays. Sometimes on Saturdays, and Sunday afternoons were never good. I began to sense a pattern. I called Tom for advice.

"So what do you think I should do?" I asked.

"I don't fucking know!" Tom replied.

"Did you like him?"

"Actually, I did," he said, "but Cindy didn't." Tom's friend Cindy however, was a well-known racist.

"Was it because he is half Cuban?"

"No, I thought that may have been it too, but she said that he just was not her cup of tea." Apparently, Cindy, as well as Tom, were to be avoided upon dating someone new. "Hey, did you watch *One Life to Live* today?" We continued talking about soap operas for about a half an hour until Kevin called on the other line. We were supposed to go to dinner with my friend Chad, who had just gotten into town.

"Hey babe, I am picking you up in an hour, are you about ready?"

"Yea, about that, I can't go," he said. I had just gotten out of a hot conversation about ABC soaps to be stood up. "Actually, this just isn't working for me. I hate to say it, but it's true. It's not you – it's me."

"Is this really happening right now?" I asked.

"Yeah, I just need to sort things out with myself right now and be alone. I am super sorry."

Super sorry? What things did Kevin really need to sort out? His drinking problem or, the fact that he had an abnormally small dick? I hung up on him. This breakup had really upset me. I did like Kevin very much and even though he was drunk when he told me, he still had told me that he loved me. Something no one else had ever said to me. Being as resilient as always, I picked myself up and went out with Chad. Suddenly, I turned into a whirling dervish – a drunken cyclone if you will – drinking my way through life for the next few weeks. As fate would have it, I bumped into Kevin six times the week after he dumped me. I ignored him until the seventh time when I saw him with another guy. They were both drunk and all over each other.

"I thought you needed time to be alone right now." I asked.

"I'm sorry Mark," Kevin replied.

"Who is he?" the gay guy with him asked.

"I am his ex-boyfriend of about a week, who are you?" I said, shaking my head from side to side.

"I'm Timmy. His boyfriend of the past nine years," the gay said.

First of all, what man out of elementary school thinks it's ok to be referred to as Timmy? Secondly, this asshole was playing both of us.

"Aren't you pissed he was seeing me, uh, Tim?" I asked.

"We were on a break," Gay Tim said.

Apparently, I was the only one being played. None of this makes any sense to me to this day. But, as I was walking out of the bar that night, I made sure to let everyone know that Kevin had the most unusually small penis I had ever seen on a grown man.

Kevin was a true blue bastard, but nothing prepared me for what was in store. Which was of course, the granddaddy of all dysfunctional relationships. After moving from New York back to Washington D.C., I began working at a small café in Adams Morgan – the absolute most obnoxious part of the absolute most obnoxious city I had ever lived in, but, the café was great. It enabled me to make friends after failing to do so after the first four months of my D.C. residency. One summer night, a few on my co-workers and I were sitting on the café patio, smoking cigarettes and drinking mimosas. I was on the clock of course, so I was trying to drink and help customers at the same time. The café was great because management was really lax and I basically got away with murder. I was working with my Russian transplant Alexy, who was a little slow on the uptake, so I would pick up his slack. I figured he was so slow because he was from Siberia and the heat of the D.C. summer confused him. At least, that was the only thing I could think of to excuse his utter incompetence. Nonetheless, I ended up picking up one of his tables where a single man was sitting alone reading what may have been the biggest book I have ever seen. I barely spoke to him because honestly, after a day of drinking mimosas in the heat and waiting tables, my conversation skills were usually below par. After the single man had paid his check, I noticed he had left me his number on the receipt. Priceless! No one had ever left me their number on a check before, and since he was pretty cute, and the summer seemed to be dragging on uneventfully, I thought I would send him a text message.

"Hey cute boy. Thanks for leaving me your number. Lets grab a drink sometime," I texted.

Immediately, I got a return text: "Yea. Maybe tomorrow"

I texted back: "Can't, working."

"Tuesday?"

"Working"

"Wednesday?"

"Wednesday, I am having margaritas at the pool all day. Maybe afterwards."

"K."

All of this texting was making me thirsty. I needed a drink.

The next day, I went about my usual business. After I left the gym, I saw that I had a message.

I checked my voicemail and listened to what had to have been one of the most hilarious and memorable messages I had ever received:

"Hey this is Jake from last night," the voice in my mailbox said. "It's nice to know that you actually have a name." I guess I had forgotten to tell him my name through text message. "Well, Mark, it's nice to know your name because I was going around calling you mystery meat." Ha, ha, ha, I laughed. "Anyway, I just wanted to call you and let you know that I am in the 'M' word." Murderer? Masochist? Mathematician? "Married" HA HA HA. "To a woman" HA HA HA!!!!!!! "And if that's ok with you, I would love to get together with you sometime this week and grab that drink. If the whole marriage thing doesn't bother you. Give me a call and let me know what you want to do."

I was dying. Before I did anything, I was going to have to change my pants because I had just peed myself. I had never heard anything as funny as that and saved it so I could play it for anyone that would listen. Who did this guy think I was? A home-wrecker? Certainly not. There was no way I was about to start dating a married man. I may be a slut, but Amy Fisher I am not.

The next day, I went to work at the café and it was business as usual until about two seconds before I was leaving and Jake sat down in my section.

"Oh hey, what are you doing here?" I asked him.

"I came to see you. You never returned my call yesterday and you said you were working tonight so I thought I would swing by," he responded.

"Dude, I don't date married guys."

"That's OK, I totally understand. Well, since I am here, I may as well have a beer." I got him a beer and since he was the only table in my section, I sat down and chatted with him for a bit. We talked and laughed until I finally asked him why, if he was married, was he after me?

"I just thought you were cute," Jake said.

"But you're married," I replied.

"Yes, but I am slowly realizing that I am not into women at all." He continued to tell me that a few months before he was on a business trip and ended up hooking up with a guy in California. He never told his wife.

"Whoa! That's crazy!" I said. "So why did you get married in the first place?" I was overwhelmed with intrigue.

"I don't know. I am from a small town in West Virginia. My wife was my best friend in high school and our parents were best friends so it just seemed to be the thing to do."

"Uh, OK," I replied. "You know, it is OK to be gay."

"I know, but I just didn't want to disappoint everyone."

Clearly, this was not an acceptable reason to get married. If someone had told me that was the reason they had married me, I would have divorced them on the spot. The more we spoke, the more I realized what a loose cannon he was. First of all, he was married to a woman and flirting with me. Secondly, he was obviously unhappy with himself. Lastly, he was a close talker. I really wanted to hear what he had to say but there was no reason for him to be all up in my business.

I finally realized that this was going nowhere and told him to pay his check so I could leave. This was normal behavior for me at the café and Jake was to be no exception. On his way out – I stopped him.

"I forgot to ask you – what do you do for a living?" I asked.

"I'm a psychiatrist," he replied, "in the Army." He walked out.

I was waiting for Ashton Kutcher to pop out and tell me that I was getting punked. Was this guy serious? He was not only a total emotional train-wreck, but also married and a therapist in the Army. I mean, he seemed nice enough, but breaking up a marriage was not really on my list of things to do in 2008. Going to the Golden Globes with Goldie Hawn, on the other hand was totally on that list.

The next day I was having my scheduled margaritas at the pool with my friend, Meg, when I got a phone call.

"Hey Mark," Dr. Jake said into the phone.

"What's up?" I asked.

"Oh nothing, just calling to see what you are doing."

"Uh, having margaritas at the pool. It's Wednesday, obvi."

"Obvi?" he asked.

"God! Obviously!" I replied. Jesus! If he was going to try and date me, the least he could have done was learned the language. "What's going on?"

"Just wanted to see if you wanted to get together." Wow, this guy was really determined. I kind of appreciated that.

"Well," I replied, "I am meeting some friends later if you want to come." Damn tequila, always lowers my inhibitions. Not to mention the bullshit filter between my brain and my mouth. I would need to switch to vodka before he met us. He agreed to meet us and I dragged Meg's drunk, sunburnt ass down the street where my sister Kim was waiting for us.

We all sat down and drank and had a gay old time until Dr. Jake walked in.

"Damn, why are all of the hot guys always gay?" Meg squawked.

"Oh, that's the married guy I was telling you about," I told her.

"You didn't tell me he was gorgeous," Meg said. After the amount of alcohol she had consumed that day, Gene Wilder would have looked like a dreamboat to her.

"I thought the fact that he was married and in the Army kind of trumped the fact that he was hot," I said.

Dr. Jake joined my sister, Meg and I as we enjoyed a few cocktails. After the girls had parted ways with us, Dr. Jake and I were left alone. I was beginning to kind of like Dr. Jake and thought that, if nothing else, we could become very good friends. Once again, my old friend Grey Goose had turned on me and before I knew it, I was in Jake's marital bed, legs in the air.

It was some of the best sex I had ever had. I don't know if it was because he was gorgeous or because it was so forbidden but it felt great. Afterwards, I didn't feel so great. How could I have done this? I had slept with a woman's husband. I was certainly not raised this way and I was in no position right now to become an army wife.

For the next week, Dr. Jake and I went back and forth. I kept telling him that I couldn't possibly be with him. There was absolutely no way that this was going to work out – there was so much against us, i.e., he was married, in the closet and in the Army. He insisted that we could make it work and after about a week, it began to make sense in my alcohol filled head. Yes, maybe we could.

Dr. Jake finally came out to his wife and moved into an apartment conveniently located two blocks away from the café. For the next few months Dr. Jake and I were inseparable. It was the best summer of my life. It was beginning to seem as thought Dr. Jake was the one, except there was a huge cloud looming over our relationship – his ex-wife.

I think he felt bad for leaving her because whenever she would call, he answered it. When we were at dinner and she called – he answered it.

When we were having sex and she called – he answered it. This was beginning to become a problem so I finally confronted him about it.

"Why do you need to take her calls all of the time?" I asked.

"Because she is my best friend and I like to hear from her," he replied.

"Even while we are having sex?"

"I just feel so bad for what I have done to her. She is my best friend."

"Well you have a new best friend now bitch and this is totally unacceptable!"

"No. I don't," he answered. "Megan is my best friend and if you have a problem with it, I am sorry."

Right. I don't think that Jake knew exactly what this relationship was doing to me. I was basically living in his ex-wife's shadow and I didn't like it. Dr. Jake had made it seem as if we were married. We spent every day and night together and were never separated except when we were working. My feelings for Jake were real but all of the secrets were starting to pile up. I had never met any of his friends because they were all in the Army and no one knew he was gay. The fact that he was still legally married and his wife was constantly calling began to become a bit too overwhelming. I felt it was time for a brief trial separation. The next week we spent separately.

Dr. Jake and I eventually did get back together. He had planned on going on vacation with his family for a week, leaving me alone in the apartment. I figured that this time away from each other would be good for us because he was smothering me and I could not breathe. He was turning into a child I had to baby-sit and he was incapable of living a life on his own. It was almost as if he had to be guided along in life. This was the perfect time for him to go on a vacation – without me.

He was gone for a week and called that Friday to tell me that he had to come home early because a hurricane or typhoon or something was nearing the beach where he was staying. I told him that I would be working that night but would see him when I got home. I did work that evening but after I was done, my boss asked me if I would join him for a drink when I had finished. I agreed, not thinking it was going to be the cause of World War III.

After the drink with my boss, I returned home and greeted Jake with a few vodka perfumed hugs and went to bed. The next morning I woke up to find Jake sitting in bed next to me, arms folded.

"I don't want to date you anymore," he said

"It's 8 am." I hadn't even had my coffee yet and this douche bag was giving me this shit?

"I know, I set my alarm," he replied.

"You set your alarm to break up with me?"

"Yes, I wanted to catch you before you went to work."

"How thoughtful of you!"

"You knew I was coming home last night and you were at the café, drinking and having a good old time."

"I was with my boss." Wait a second. How the hell did he even know that? Did he implant a tracking device on me? "How did you know I was having a drink with my boss last night? Who, by the way, I don't even like that much. He asked me to help him out with something."

"Whatever, I went by last night and saw you sitting there."

"Why didn't you come in?"

"I was mad."

"You're a borderline stalker. What the hell is wrong with you? I couldn't say 'no' to my boss."

"Yes, you could have. I haven't seen you in a week."

"Big fucking deal Jake, we aren't married. I am NOT your wife." Not only had he set his alarm to break up with me, now he was stalking me and pissing me off in general.

"I don't want to do this with you anymore," he said.

"Fine," I said. "I have to go to work now." I got in the shower and went to work. I guess I was ready for this relationship to be over, because I didn't seem to care all that much that we were no longer together. I really cared for Jake, but he was a mess and I was increasingly becoming messier. However, our story does not end there. In my usual destructive fashion, I continued seeing Jake after we broke up. My drinking had taken a dangerous turn and I was really beginning to get out of hand. I tried to stop talking to Jake and I tried to stop drinking but nothing worked. He kept popping up everywhere and in order to deal with him, I needed to medicate myself. On one particular night, I bumped into him outside of a drug store.

"Oh, hey," Jake said as I bumped into him, "funny meeting you here."

"Yea. What are you doing here?"

"Just walking home," he said. "Wow, I wish this drug store was around when I was making out with that kid the other night. If I had had some condoms I totally would have fucked him."

"Are you serious?" I asked.

He was. I could not believe this. Who says that to someone they just broke up with? Someone they broke up with at eight o'clock in the morning nonetheless. Was he for real or was he just socially retarded? Perhaps it was the four glasses of wine I had had before bumping into him, or my sheer disgust at his comment, but something had come over me and I ended up punching him in the neck. I was aiming for his face, but after four glasses of wine, I thought that was a pretty good shot.

Jake eventually apologized and we tried to become friends, but it never really worked for me. I was very hurt by everything that had happened between us and my drinking was reaching its breaking point. One night when Jake and I were supposed to get together, I ended up drinking all night and showed up at his apartment at five in the morning. The next day, I woke up in Jake's bed at five in the afternoon.

"I think I have a drinking problem," I told him as the room around him was spinning.

"Really?" He acted as if he was surprised; as if I had just told him I was pregnant with his baby.

"Well Jake, I did try to crawl through your window to get into your apartment last night," I said. " That's not the point of entry a normal person uses when trying to enter someone else's home. Don't you think I have a problem?" I asked, thinking Jake, a therapist would be able to help me. Since he was once my boyfriend, I figured he would at least be willing to help me.

"Not really," he replied. "I think you're OK."

It was then that I realized that Dr. Jake was an emotional mess and I was an even bigger one. It made him feel better about himself to have me come around because seeing me, an even bigger mess than he, made him feel better about his ridiculous life. I knew that I could not continue seeing Dr. Jake as he was bringing me down and I knew that I had to get help with my drinking.

I did get help with my drinking but Dr. Jake did not stop. He was determined to bring me down, make me miserable and fail and what I was doing. I finally had to threaten him with a restraining order to get him to stop contacting me. This relationship really hurt me. Someone who told me they loved me was clearly going out of their way to hurt me and bring me down. I could not believe that a therapist would tell anyone who drank every single day and tried crawling through their very own window that they did not have a drinking problem.

While these relationships all had their ridiculous circumstances, I did take something away from each and every one of them. Whether it be the dangers of looking at porn on the internet while high on crystal meth or dating a married man in the Army, I have taken everything I have learned and tried to apply it to my everyday life. I thank all of my former beaus for everything they taught me. But most of all, I would like to thank alcohol. Without you, none of these stories would have ever been possible; with you, none of these stories would have ever been told.

ADVENTURES IN SOBRIETY

Imagine a summer filled with fabulous trips to the beach, weekend excursions to the mountains and a fabulous group of friends that hung on your every word. Imagine having a successful doctor as a boyfriend and having the best sex of your life. Imagine if you will, living in a world without any consequences and having the time of your life. Now imagine, not remembering half of it.

By the summer of 2008, my drinking had taken on a life of its own. I was constantly partying and carrying on, while ignoring the important aspects of my life. I felt I had tried to make it work in D.C., where I was living at the time, but the two of us were simply not a fit. I am a New Yorker after all, and as far as I am concerned, there is nowhere else to live. I had moved to D.C. on a whim and after less than a year, I was done. My real friends were in New York and I knew if I had just put forth a little more effort, I would be back where I belonged, living the life I had always imagined I would lead. But the truth was, I had more than enough time and plenty of opportunities to have that life and ended up pissing it away either by making bad decisions or conducting inappropriate behavior wherever I went. I had all but given up any dream of returning to New York. I would talk about moving back, and take an occasional interview, but I was not putting forth the effort required to make a happy life for myself. I was twenty-five years old, waiting tables and not doing much to become the respected adult that I thought I deserved to be. My life had turned into a constant bar crawl, hopping from bar to bar, flirting with acquaintances and making false promises to myself, and everyone around me. The only thing I began looking forward to was having that first drink, but one drink always led to many and in a short time it became clear to everyone around me that a problem was brewing, literally.

The final night of my nine-month bar crawl in D.C., and what I hope to be the final night I ever drank, was one of the most embarrassing nights of my life. It was a Saturday in October and I was pulling a double at the café. In the morning, we were serving brunch, but that night, we were hosting the Miss Adams Morgan Day Pageant. The Miss Adams Morgan Day Pageant is a yearly event that brings drag queens from around the world to Washington D.C. to compete for the prize of Miss Adams Morgan. I am not exactly sure what this entails (I think they win a years supply of hairspray and a Sham-Wow or something lame like that), but it is a pretty big deal for the area and everyone said it was to be the party of the year. I was not happy to be working, as usual. It really took away from my drinking schedule, which on nice days such as this one included drinking outside. So instead of drinking outside and relaxing, I decided to drink on the job. This was not untypical of Saturday afternoons. The café was pretty slow, so the staff would drink during the day and usually party at night. I had to work that night, and knowing that should have been the first clue not to start drinking. I began drinking early in the afternoon that fateful Saturday and didn't stop until five o'clock the next morning. As the night rolled on, I kept drinking, even though I had already blacked out. I was serving tables in a dress (I figured I had to be in costume, since the drag queens were in town) and did not remember anything. I was handling money that wasn't mine and serving people in platform heels. The next day when I went back to apologize for my ridiculous behavior, as I had done so many times before, no one seemed to pay any mind to what had gone. "Oh don't worry about it Mark," one of my co-workers said. "We're used to it with you." I couldn't take it anymore. Is this what people really thought of me? How was it possible for me to make a life for myself if I continued to behave like this? I knew I had to stop drinking once and for all and knew I could not do it by myself. This had gone on for too long and it was time for it to end. I looked up a place online that could help me and went there that day. For the next thirty days, I struggled to find my true self and get rid of the alcohol in my system.

DAY ONE

It's always funny to me that AA meetings are always liquor store adjacent. It's like when you are going to a gym that has a McDonald's in the basement. My new AA meeting was two doors down from a liquor store and I pondered what door to walk through. I picked the AA meeting, knowing what I had to do and walked up the stairs. But after every step I took up, I took two steps back down.

"Do I really want to do this?" I thought as I clutched the handrail. "Think of all of the fun times I am going to miss. Halloween is right around the corner, then Thanksgiving, Election Day, Christmas, my birthday, Kwanza, Boxing Day, New Years Eve, all perfect days to be drunk off my ass. What about Mary's party this weekend? I couldn't possibly go there and not drink. That would be so rude of me." I had walked up and down the stairs about fifty-five times in twenty minutes. Anyone looking at me would have thought I was rehearsing for a Paula Abdul video. I felt as if there was no way I was going be able to do this because not drinking seemed impossible to me. Everything in my life at that point seemed to revolve around drinking. More importantly, I had just found out that I could mix my two favorite things, iced tea and vodka together and felt duty bound to spread the word about my latest creation! I was going to miss all of the fun if I stopped now. I didn't realize at the time that the fun had actually stopped for me months ago.

I didn't know what to do. I sat on the bottom steps of the local AA meeting and thought about whether or not I really needed to go up the stairs. After about ten more minutes of fighting the demons in my head, I figured I would go upstairs and see what this program was all about. Maybe after hearing a little bit more about what was going on, I could decide whether or not I needed to be there. Besides, I had already told anyone who would listen that I had joined AA (even though at that point I had not) so that it would seem as if I had gotten a handle on my problem. "Damn it!" I thought. I had to do this now or I would look like a complete asshole. Maybe I told everyone I was joining AA so that I would *actually* do something. I determined it would be the best thing to do for now, and if I did not like it, I would just quit, like I had done so many times before.

I went up the stairs and before I entered the room there was one more step and a sign above it that read: STEP ONE. "Whatever," I thought. I was still hung-over from two days before. I figured I would just apply my blasé attitude to this, as I had done with everything else in my life, and be done with it. I took a seat next to a man would looked like he was homeless. He was wearing a huge blue coat with a fur-lined hood. He had to be one of the oldest human beings still around. I knew that a lot of Veterans were alcoholics. Perhaps, he had fought in the war-between-the-states.

I sat and tried to focus on what everyone was saying. I kept quiet, even when they asked if there was anyone new to the group. I really didn't want to be associated with any of these people so I didn't say a word. I was really just giving this program a "test drive" to see what it was all about. I didn't need to make friends just yet. Just remain anonymous until it suited me to make my presence known.

The meeting continued on and I looked around the room. There were people from every walk of life imaginable. Homemakers, lawyers, cab drivers, businessmen, government officials, black, white, gay, straight, male, female, all of these people were bonded by their common weakness – alcohol. There was an older lady who was very well dressed - in driving gloves and all - who looked so glamorous, sitting next to a man who was missing a tooth. She did not seem to mind that the man next to her had possibly just eaten out of a dumpster. This woman looked like someone I would have liked to have partied with. She looked like she was born with a rocks glass in her hand.

The meeting ended. I had not really listened to anything that anyone had to say because I was fascinated by all of the people who were around me. Instead of asking someone for help, or sticking around to learn more about the program, I bolted. I went home and decided to call my uncle, who had been in the program for over twenty years.

"Best thing I ever did," my uncle said into the phone.

"Yes, but I am not sure I actually have a problem," I said.

"Why did you go to an AA meeting if you do not think you have a problem?"

"Because I got really drunk the other night and didn't want to look like a complete asshole, but did want to make it look like I was getting a hold of my life."

"Why don't you just get a hold of your life?" That seemed like a really hard thing to do at this point. I didn't know if I was actually ready to get my shit together. But talking about it, at least made it seem as if I did. "Do you remember talking to me about this a few years ago?" my uncle asked. He was referring to the time I called him after drinking a bottle of Jack Daniels and asked him who I needed to fuck to join AA.

"I think so," I replied.

"No, you don't, you were drunk." He knew I was lying. "If you think you have a drinking problem, then you most likely do," he continued. "Normal people who drink every so often usually don't think they have a drinking problem. Do you ever blackout?"

I hesitated to answer.

"I'll take that as a 'yes'. Mark, why don't you take this test online? It takes five minutes and if you answer more than three of the questions with a 'yes' just call me back."

My uncle gave me the website to check out and I looked over the questions, dreading what the outcome of this questionnaire would be. I scrolled down to get to the body of the page and read:

Do you ever blackout?

This wasn't a hard one, as I had blacked out three times the previous week. I answered "yes."

Do you ever drink more than anyone around you?

Since at this point I had been drinking with hardcore drinkers all summer, I chose to answer this question "maybe." Due to my surroundings, I felt a "yes" would be misconstrued.

Do you ever crave a drink?

Damn it! This wasn't looking good. Two "yes" and one "maybe."

Do you ever leave your house with the intent to get drunk?

Three "yes" and one "maybe."

Do you ever lie about drinking?

There were fifteen questions left, but I was done with this test. I turned away from the computer in shame and noticed that my uncle was calling my cell, so I picked it up.

"Did you take the test?" my uncle asked

"Yeah, I didn't get very far though. I got four "yes" and a maybe," I said thinking that was something to be proud of.

"A 'maybe'?" he asked. "Only you could take a yes or no test and come up with a maybe. How many questions did you get through?"

"Five," I replied.

"Ok, it's a twenty question quiz and if you answer more than three with a 'yes' they suggest that you seek help." Tests were never fun, but this one, in particular really blew. "Do me a favor," he continued, "Go back to the meetings and see if you can go without drinking for the next week. If you have trouble, just give me a call."

I hung up and felt a little better. At least my uncle would be my friend if I stopped drinking. Maybe we could go to the movies on Friday nights and do fun things like those ladies who wear red hats. I went to bed and decided I would take my uncle's advice and go back to a meeting tomorrow and see if I could stop drinking for a week. As I was falling asleep, my pseudo boyfriend Dr. Jake called.

"How was your day?" he asked over the phone.

"Fine," I replied. "I went to AA."

"Really?" he said acting surprised.

"Yeah, I am pretty sure that I need to be there, it just seems like a pain in the ass," I said. "Did you know you have to go there everyday?"

"Well, yes. I had to go to AA meetings when I was in school. Every therapist has to."

"It's kind of boring, but there was this really pretty blonde girl there that looked like someone who I would have gotten wasted with all the time." I loved getting drunk with pretty girls and telling them how pretty they were. It's no wonder girls love hanging out with gay guys.

"Well, keep at it and let me know if you need anything," he said.

"Goodnight," I said and hung up the phone. Was I going to have to give up Nyquil as well? I was having a bitch of a time getting to bed that night. I mean, I wasn't about to pull a Kitty Dukakis or anything, but I wasn't sure of what the rules regarding sleep aides were.

DAY TWO

I went back to the meeting the next day and found that I had little trouble getting up the stairs this time. I had already been there once, so I figured that I didn't look like a complete douche bag sitting in a room filled with strangers talking about drinking. I sat and watched everyone come in and noticed that a pretty girl, who was definitely a lesbian, took the big seat in the middle. Her name was Laura and she was to be leading the group today. She was exactly how I liked my lesbians. She was tattooed and pierced everywhere imaginable and also looked like she had a really awful attitude. I thought I would have to talk to her later, as she looked like someone who was perfect to make fun of others with. Laura sat down and told her story. Although she was a lesbian, she was once married to a man named Luke.

"How perfect!" I thought. "Just like Luke and Laura on *General Hospital*." Except the Laura on TV was not a lesbian and the Laura who sat before me had probably not gone around the world looking for the Ice Princess. Nevertheless, it guaranteed that I would at least remember her name. Laura began her story and told the group that she had began drinking when she was a teenager. She had always known that she was a lesbian but got married to a man because she thought it was the right thing to do. All I could think of was Dr. Jake. He had done pretty much the same thing and was now kind of dating me. Funny how that works out, the whole *I'm-gay-but-I-am-going-to-marry-someone-from-the-opposite-sex* thing. As Laura continued her story, I realized how similar we were. She said that she drank to make herself feel better, which was something I had down to an art form. She drank to celebrate. She drank when she was depressed. She drank when she was alone. She drank when people were around her. She drank because it was there. I was enthralled by her story because it was as if she was telling my story. After the meeting, I needed to know more about this woman.

"Hey girl!" I said. It's a good thing I know the lesbian lingo. "I really liked what you had to say."

"Thank you," she replied.

"It was almost as if you were telling my story. You and I are like the same person. Except, you are a lesbian, and I of course, I am not."

She laughed. "Well, if you hang around here long enough, you will see that we all have the same story."

"Really?" I asked. I looked around the room at the faces that stood before me. There was a guy with dreadlocks who sat in the corner staring at the floor while twitching. I had not been in the group for very long, but I was there long enough to know that I was going to be calling that guy "Twitch." There was no way that Twitch and I had the same story. We're so different - I flat iron my hair.

Laura could see the confusion in my eyes. "Yeah!" she yelled. "We're all a bunch of fucking drunks!" She laughed. I didn't think that this remark was all that funny but I gave her an awkward half smile anyway. Lesbians are notoriously unfunny so I thought I would throw her a bone. "Here's my number if you need anything," she said as she handed me her card. "Please, feel free to call anytime."

"Thanks," I said. I was certainly confused as to why this nice lesbian was giving me her number so I replied, "I have a lesbian sister." She smiled and walked away.

I felt a lot better after leaving my second AA meeting. If Laura could get sober, and her story was just about the same as mine, maybe I could do this after all. I went to the café right after the meeting. I was told by my uncle that working at a place that served alcohol was not a good idea especially during your first month of sobriety. I told him that unless he wanted to support me through this tough economic time, I didn't really have much of a choice. But I hated waiting tables. It felt like I had done it for so long and the only thing that made it bearable was the fact that I could get shit faced drunk for free. Now that option no longer existed so it just became something I had to do in order to survive. At the very least, I had made a few good friends during my time there and it was always good to see them. I walked into the café feeling relieved and really good about my new endeavor.

"Hey Mark," my boss said as I walked in. "How's rehab?"

"Excuse me?" I replied.

"I thought you went to rehab?"

"Um, no. Had I gone to rehab, I would have been gone for at least a month. I just didn't work yesterday so maybe you got confused. I am in AA now."

"Right," he said. "I am very proud of you," he continued as he knocked back the remains of his vodka cranberry at four in the afternoon on a Tuesday. "You really needed it."

I breezed past him and walked in the coatroom to gather myself. How could my boss, a man never seen without a cocktail in his hand possibly tell me that I needed to go to AA? He needed to go to AA. I went on a whim and I am only there for the duration of the week to see if I actually can do it.

I went about the rest of my day on a pink cloud. As I served my customers their drinks and they proceeded to get drunker and drunker, I realized how obnoxious I must have been while I was drinking. I flashed back to a few years earlier when I was out drinking with my roommates. We had been drinking all night at our favorite local bar and I pulled my usual *leave-without-saying-goodbye* move. The good old Irish goodbye. About an hour later, they found me asleep in a vegetable stand across the street from our apartment. My roommates had to literally pick me up and carry me home. Every time I would get drunk, my life warped into *Weekend at Bernie's*. My friends would have to carry my seemingly lifeless body from the bar back home. We all know *Weekend at Bernie's* was fun for no one. I was glad that I wouldn't have to go through that again – at least not this week. I went to bed that night feeling much better. Maybe I could do this after all.

DAY THREE

This morning Dr. Jake called and told me that he was going to New York that weekend and asked me if I wanted to go. He said he was going up on business and if I wanted to come, he would have some time to see shows and go out for dinner and such. I declined but thanked him for the invitation. I was really feeling good about this AA thing and told him I thought it was best if I stayed in D.C. for the time being, but I told him to be good. It was true that Dr. Jake and I were no longer dating, but I told him that I thought it was best for him to not sleep with anyone while I was going through my first days of sobriety.

In typical Mark fashion, my problem was quickly becoming everyone else's. True, Dr. Jake and I were no longer dating, but we were acting as if we were and it would really piss me off if he slept with someone else at this point. There was still a glimmer of hope of getting back together, even though he set his alarm to break up with me. I told him that it would be best for my recovery if he didn't sleep with anyone else and he agreed not to.

The fact that he was going to New York without me annoyed me nonetheless. I knew that he would be going out and having fun without me, and the thought of that made me want to scream. I still could not understand why everyone else seemed to be having fun but me. I was coming to terms with the fact that I did have a problem, but why did this have to be so boring? Everyone from the café had gone out the night before and I knew they were going to have amazing stories to tell me. Tuesday Booze days were always memorable evenings and I had just missed one. I felt sorry for myself so I went to an AA meeting and thought maybe someone else would feel sorry for me there.

I found it very hard to listen to anything that anyone had to say that day. Instead I once again took a look around the room at the faces that stared back. I noticed the old man in the blue jacket was back. I also noticed that an elderly gay man, who bared a shocking resemblance to Palmer Courtlandt from *All My Children*, joined him today. I decided I would refer to him as Palmer Courtlandt forever. I saw that the older well-dressed woman was back. Today she was wearing a pillbox hat. I decided that I would refer to her from then on as Bunny McDougall. She did, after all, look like Charlotte's mother-in-law from *Sex and the City*. Finally, I saw a little red haired girl in the corner who would heretofore be referred to as little orphan Annie. I could not pay attention to anything because of the cast of characters that surrounded me.

After the meeting, little orphan Annie came up to me.

"Hey, are you new here?" Annie asked.

"Yep," I said.

"Wow. We are like the youngest ones here," she said.

"Yea, right?"

"My name is sjkdhaskjdfh," she said. I still to this day do not remember her name. I have since spoken to her on several different occasions. I know what street she lives on and what her major in college is, but can't for the life of me remember her name. I just got so used to calling her Annie, that it became all I could remember her by. "Today has been really troubling for me," Annie said. "I have finals and I am really flipping out." She continued to talk but I really wasn't listening. Why on earth did this girl come over and start talking to me? I really was not interested in anything she had to say. All I wanted to do was ask her where the hell Bernadette Peters was and whatever happened to that frigging dog of hers. She finally said goodbye and gave me her number and told me to call her if I needed anything. I put her in my phone under L.O. Annie. Why on earth were so many people giving me their numbers? I had no idea, but all I could think of as I left my meeting that day was *WE GOT ANNIE!!!*

DAY FOUR

Today I woke up feeling like shit. It was as if the hangover from the Miss Adams Morgan Day event had not gone away. I didn't want to get out of bed. I knew I had to go to work eventually, but I did not have to be there until 6 pm so essentially I could sleep all day then roll into work. But something inside of me was telling me to get up, go to a meeting, go to the gym, eat a healthy lunch and get on with my day. My body was telling me to lie in bed all day and watch my stories, but my head was telling me to get up and have a productive day. After all, I could watch my stories on the treadmill, which killed two birds with one stone.

I did end up going to an AA meeting that day. I told myself upon entering the room that I was going to pay attention to what everyone was saying and not cast a musical in my head. I looked around the room once I sat down. I saw Twitch was there. Sitting a few seats down with him was Bunny McDougall. She was talking to Palmer Courtlandt. I wondered if they were friends. Maybe they went to Happy Hour together after the meetings. I tried focusing on AA. Today was the day that I was going to finally get something out of what all of these people were talking about. As the meeting was getting started, a big, 50-something homosexual sat down in the chair in the middle.

"Hi everyone. My name is Michael and I am an alcoholic," the man said. I could see myself turning into Michael in about twenty-five years. He seemed fairly successful by the clothes he was wearing and extremely outgoing. But he also seemed like he had a really bad attitude, something I could appreciate even more.

"Actually," Michael continued, "I am a huge fucking drunk!"

This was amazing. Now we're getting down to the nitty-gritty. Michael told his story and I was utterly fascinated by it. He was from New York, just like me. He had been a very successful doctor up there, but something had always bothered him. He, like Laura Lesbian and Dr. Jake, had married someone of the opposite sex knowing he was a homosexual. He was a twin and felt as if his parents always had favored his twin brother over him. I felt his pain. I was one of five children and at this point, I felt as if my parents had all but given up on me. I had completed college, but I had not accomplished much more than that. My brothers and sisters all had careers and families and I really didn't have much besides some really good drinking buddies and an incredible knowledge of show-tunes. Michael continued his story and told the group how he would order a case of scotch every month and drink each and every bottle in the case. He began drinking all of the time and almost lost his medical license. But something inside of him told him that he needed to get help and he did. He had been sober for over twenty years now and I found myself really respecting him. He had dragged himself up by his coat tails and made a much better life for himself. He told the group that every day that we did not drink was a great day because we hadn't taken a drink. I was inspired by what he had to say and hung on every word that came out of his mouth. I think had I paid attention to what anyone was saying in the first four days, I would have learned something but I was too busy making up ridiculous nicknames for people.

After the meeting, I left in my usual *dine and dash* fashion. There was a lot to take in from what I had just heard and I needed some time to reflect and smoke about ten cigarettes. I may have stopped drinking, but my smoking had taken on a life of its own. Perhaps I was replacing one with the other, I was smoking as if someone had told me it was now a healthy thing to do. As I lit up a cigarette and walked down the street, I heard someone following me.

"Hey!" Michael yelled. "Wait up." I turned around and saw that Michael was running toward me. I stopped and turned around to face him, inadvertently blowing smoke in his face. "What's you name?"

"Mark," I replied.

"I have seen you coming around for the past few days. I am assuming you are new."

"Yep. Day four."

Michael's eyes lit up. "That's great." He opened his arms and pulled me into a huge bear hug. What the hell was wrong with all of these people? Why were they so happy all of the time? Was there some sort of punch everyone was drinking except for me, and if so, was it filled with vodka? "You remind me of myself at your age." This was surprising as I had not said but two words to him and he didn't in fact know my age.

"What do you mean?" I said dragging on my cigarette.

"I saw you in the meeting," he replied. Oh shit. What was I doing? Picking my nose? Farting and not knowing about it? "You sat there – did not say a word and ran out of the meeting as soon as it was over. You probably think this whole program is bullshit don't you?"

"Well…"

"You do. I am sure of it." Could this guy read minds? If so, he was right on the money. "I did too when I started. I sat in the room thinking 'what the fuck are these people talking about?' I didn't think I belonged and I thought that everyone around me was weird. But if you stick with it, I promise, it will change your life."

I looked at him and saw what he would have looked like, had he kept drinking the way he told the group he had been. Thirty years of drinking a bottle of scotch every night would probably have done a number on him. His hair would have most likely been gone. His eyes would have been sagging and most likely would not have had the physic he presently had, but a huge beer belly. I looked into what I imagined drunken Michael's face would have looked like and realized that if I kept drinking the way I had been, I would have ended up looking like a complete mess. I needed to stop drinking for my vanity if nothing else.

"Just keep coming back," he said. "Anyone can do it – and we are all in this together."

I felt like someone finally had my back. He told me to take his number and to call him if I needed anything.

"Why the fuck do people keep giving me their numbers?" I asked.

"Because like I said we are all in this together. Whatever you are going through now, someone has most likely gone through it before. Alcoholics help other alcoholics because no one can understand what you are really feeling except someone who has gone through this shit before," he replied. Finally, someone explained to me why I had all of these first names with last initials in my phone. These people were here to help me. It was starting to make some sense. I thanked Michael and we hugged. All of this hugging was tiring me out. It was time for another cigarette. As I lit up, I noticed Bunny McDougall and Palmer Courtlandt, walking down the street in the other direction.

"Hey, Michael," I asked. "What's with those two?"

Michael looked towards the two people I had hoped most to befriend in the group. "Oh, the daughters of the American Revolution? I don't know," he said. "They have been in the program since the British invaded D.C. and burned down the White House." He laughed and turned to walk away. I was so happy that Michael had talked to me. I felt that I now had a real friend in the program and could succeed in this.

I had used alcohol to deal with people and soon realized that everyone around me was beginning to annoy the absolute shit out of me. People were not even doing huge things to irritate me. Stupid shit like holding up the subway or looking at me the wrong way aggravated me to no end. But the worst was waiting tables. Anything that anyone asked of me seemed to be a huge inconvenience. "May I please have some salt?" a customer would ask. "Why don't you get it your fucking self?" I would think. People seemed to be even more demanding than usual, but it wasn't true. No one was asking for anything out of the ordinary.

After all, I was there to wait on people. It seemed as if the world was against me, but on that day, I was pushed a little too far.

I went to the café after my meeting and it seemed to be business as usual. Boring, homely people were sitting around talking about politics, hoping that someone was eavesdropping on their conversation and thinking they were smart. I was waiting on a lovely couple with whom I had made my usual jokes with. They were soon joined by a little Asian woman who could have fit in my pocket, and her huge six-foot-three inch black boyfriend. Talk about an odd couple, it was like the Notorious B.I.G. had just rolled into the restaurant with Mulan. They sat down and I took their order. I walked back to put their order in the computer and walked by their table once more, heading to another table when the Asian woman stopped me.

"Is my food ready yet?" she asked.

"Are you serious?" I replied. It had been less than a minute since I had last seen her.

"Yes. I am really hungry."

"Well, they actually have to cook the food so it takes some time." She winced and I walked away to take another table's order. As I was walking back toward the cute couple and their obnoxious friends, Mulan flagged me down again.

"Do you think my food is ready yet?" she asked again.

"Seriously?" I replied. "I have not even walked back to the kitchen yet. You just saw me taking that other table's order. How could your food possibly be ready yet?"

"I don't know. I am just really hungry." The cute couple looked at me with that *we're sorry* face, realizing that their friend's behavior was a little ridiculous. I couldn't even justify her response with an answer so I just walked away. I put the other table's order into the computer and walked by the Asian girl and the cute couple once again and was stopped by the famished girl.

"Do you think my food is ready yet?" she asked once more. This had all taken place in a time span of less than two minutes. Unless the Iron Chef was in the kitchen that afternoon there was no way her food could have possibly been ready.

"You do realize they have to actually cook the food, right?" I asked.

"Yes, but I am just really hungry."

I had enough. Maybe the cute couple was not as nice as I once thought they were. Maybe they were against me as well. I looked at the Asian girl and was overcome with rage. I had not taken a drink in four days and who better to take my anger out on than the little woman who apparently had not eaten at all this month.

"Maybe if you ask me one more fucking time, your food will come out faster," I yelled. She looked at me as if I had just told her she had miscarried her child. I thought she was going to cry and I walked away. What was wrong with this girl? I told the kitchen to take as long as possible to prepare her food just to piss her off. If I was suffering, she had to as well. I could sense there was some tension between me and my once friends. We did not speak much after I delivered their food, but they did leave me a huge tip. I figured they knew I was having a really bad day. I don't know where all of this irritability came from, but I knew I didn't like it. I was such a happy person before I stopped drinking, or at least I thought I was. Now I was a walking train wreck.

I went home that night and tried to go to bed but I got a text message from Dr. Jake just before dozing off.

"Off to NYC tomorrow, keep up the good work." It said. That pissed me off even more. I lay there and stewed until I finally feel asleep at 4am.

DAY FIVE

I don't know why I let Dr. Jake bother me as much as he did for those first few days of sobriety. He had set his alarm and broke up with me so that should have been the end of it. However, I am an avid watcher of soap operas and on TV, the characters in these shows tend to drag things on for as long as possible. I thought that maybe things would work out for the two of us and we would get back together. Either that or I would end up pushing him off of a cliff and having to plead insanity in court. Either way, Dr. Jake was still in my life at that point. I thought it might be a good idea to keep him around because he was, after all, a therapist and I could confide in him things I could not tell anyone else. We had also dated so he knew me very well and would support me in my latest plan. After all, he was present for most of my summer of binge drinking and saw how much I drank so I thought he might be supportive in my plight.

Dr. Jake and I were really not a good match. He was a therapist in the Army and I was a waiter. He had gone to school for several years and was really interested in what he did. He also was going through a messy divorce with his wife and decided to put me in the middle of it. He had just come out of the closet and was fascinated with the gay lifestyle, which he was just opening his eyes to see. We would go out to bars and it was if he finally felt free. Having come out several years prior, hanging out with other guys who thought the same was as I did, was not as exciting for me. It was what I had been doing for eight years and the novelty of it had already worn off on me. But every day was a new experience for him and he embraced it. Once we ended our relationship, I told him that he needed to go out and experience life for himself and to sleep with as many people as possible. I did not really mean that, but figured if he had gotten an STD or something, then he could fully appreciate the gay lifestyle.

I went to AA that day and listened to everything that was said. Little orphan Annie was there again. Today, she looked really sad. I told myself that I was going to try and be nice to the people around me. After all, we were there to help each other and I couldn't possibly go on just taking help from people and not returning it. During the meeting, the speaker, a woman named Jean, went on and told her story. She was a scientist and a raging alchy. Jean would go to work every single day and try to figure out what formulas she could mix with the solutions she had available, that would give her the same results as drinking liquor. She managed to find one that didn't kill her and she went on for about four years drinking potions in her lab. One day she finally hit bottom when she almost killed someone with a mixture she had concocted. She then went to AA and never looked back. That was nineteen years ago. She continued to take, what they call in AA, "personal inventory" and began to weed out the bad influences in her life. Jean had pretty much gotten rid of everyone who was a negative influence in her life, including her old drinking buddies and most importantly, her ex-husband. All of these people were bringing her down and having them around was hindering her recovery. Now a majority of her friends were in the program and she had never been happier.

I was once again forced to look around the room. Were these the people I was going to be associating myself with for the rest of my life? Was I destined to share a three-bedroom house in Adams Morgan with Twitch and little orphan Annie? That's really an episode of *Three's Company* that I would have skipped, but Bunny McDougal and Palmer Courtlandt could have totally played the Ropers. After the meeting, I saw Big Gay Mike and he handed me a card.

"What's this for?" I asked.

"Oh, it's just a card for you. To celebrate your first five days," he replied.

I thought this was a very nice gesture. I also hoped Big Gay Mike was not trying to hit on me. I like new friends as much as the next guy but he could have totally been my father's age.

"Just a little encouragement to help you along," he said and walked away. I saw little orphan Annie approaching me as Big Gay Mike was walking away. I gave her the *I-gotta-run-I-am-late-for-something* look and bolted. I still did not remember her name and didn't want to look like a complete asshole.

I walked onto the street and opened Mike's card, in hopes there was a gift certificate to the liquor store. "YOU DID IT! CONGRATS!!!" it said with a little dog wearing a party hat and holding a fist full of balloons. The inside of the card read, "Congrats Mark. Five days is a huge accomplishment. You should be very proud of yourself! Mike." How sweet it was to know someone had my back in case we got into a gang war with a rival AA group. But, it had only been *five* days. I had not seen Dr. Jake and no one had annoyed me to the point of running off and drinking a liter of Ketel One. This hadn't been *that* hard. I wasn't really craving a drink and was starting to feel like a normal human being. Five days was not that long of a time to stay sober for me, because most of my drinking had been done on the weekends. Since it was Friday, I decided my real goal was to make it through the weekend without drinking and that would be a real accomplishment. One week was better than five days. I figured if I turned this into a form of gambling, I could really get things done, and then if I got to one month, I got a chip, which was essentially just like gambling. After one year I would have twelve chips. That would be twelve more than when I started. Maybe an impromptu trip to Atlantic City would cure what ailed me. But for now, it was off to the café and a weekend full of waiting tables on stuck up little brats.

Friday went off without a hitch. I did not drink any alcohol; instead I rediscovered my love of Shirley Temples. I went home and went to bed. As my head hit the pillow, I realized that I had not heard from Dr. Jake at all that day. Maybe he was sleeping with someone else in New York. Maybe he was partying his face off and having the time of his life. All of these scenarios played out in my head and I once again fell asleep after 4 a.m. This sobriety thing was really doing a number on my sleeping schedule.

DAYS SIX AND SEVEN

The first weekend of sobriety was a blur. I pretty much went through the motions of being a human being, but did not show any human emotions other than anger. I had told everyone that I was in AA now and was not going to be up for going out and getting hammered anymore. I had really not grasped the "Anonymous" part of Alcoholics Anonymous. I had told anyone who would listen that I was in the program now, as if it was something to be proud of. "Guess what everyone – I am a huge drunk!" I told customers I was waiting on, homeless people on the street and pretty much anyone I encountered. "Don't bother asking me if I want a drink," I remember telling a woman asking me which way the subway was, "cause I am in the program now!" Alcohol had turned into a way for me to deal with everyday life at that point. Waiting tables was not what I had spent four years in college to do and I hated every minute of it. Drinking at the end of my shift was what I had always looked forward to. It helped me cope with the fact that I was not living the life I felt I deserved. After dealing with people I felt were beneath me all day, a nice bottle of wine really cured what ailed me.

It was Saturday and I was ready for a weekend of work. Every weekend, I worked both Saturday and Sunday brunch. This was what I imagined hell on earth to be. People were a lot moodier in the mornings and always seemed to be in some sort of rush to get off to their super busy day. During the weekend, I would always remember my brunches in New York. Brunches that would last for hours, drinking mimosas and Bloody Marys while sitting around talking with friends and having a blast. It seemed as though this never happened in D.C. People were so boring down here. They would instead, drink coffee, make the usual small talk about politics to make themselves feel smart and run off to do something lame like spend the day reading the New Yorker magazine from cover to cover and wishing they lived anywhere other than here. Everyone in D.C. annoyed the shit out of me and weekend brunches were when the worst people came out.

Saturday brunch went on without too much annoyance. I began to realize that getting people Tabasco sauce and delivering them their food, was in fact my job and why people would leave me tips, so I attempted to be nice and it really paid off. People would smile back at me when I was nice to them. What a difference a good attitude made.

On Sunday I woke up feeling relaxed and ready to grab the day by the balls and live it to its fullest. But the café was crowded that day and people seemed extra anxious to get their food and get on with their day. People were being even more demanding than usual and pissing me off. Finally, three girls sat in my section, determined to throw me off the wagon. I approached them, trying to be nice, but it seemed as though they had come to the restaurant with the intent to piss me off.

"How are you gorgeous ladies doing?" I asked. The three of them looked at me as if I had just punched each one them in the face. That was to be the first and only time I would compliment any of them. They had grabbed Bloody Marys at the bar as they were waiting for a table, and the tallest of the three girls was wincing at each sip she took.

"This Bloody Mary tastes funny to me," the tall girl with a broken Russian accent said.

"That's odd," I replied. Having made the Bloody Mary mix myself, I thought it to be one of my better batches. It was grandma's recipe for Christ's sake. The Rusky had thought otherwise. "Do you like Bloody Marys?"

"Not really," she replied.

Then why did you order a fucking Bloody Mary? I thought.

"Maybe you just got a bad one," I replied thinking this was impossible, as her two friends were drinking the exact same drink and not complaining. Since I was going to be a nice person today I offered to get her another one as if this was going to make a difference. I walked back to the bar and saw my co-worker Kate standing there.

"CUNT ALERT!" I screamed into Kate's ear. Kate was great because she had the same *go-fuck-yourself* attitude and she hated waiting on girls as much as I did. Girls seemed super-demanding. I think it had something to do with the lack of men in D.C. and the fact that most girls hadn't gotten laid in over a decade. So being annoyed by their involuntary celibacy, they would come into the café with the intent of aggravating the shit out of my co-workers and I. I got the Russian a new Bloody Mary and delivered it to their table. She sipped it and winced again. I figured that since I had made the correct attempts in rectifying the situation, it was no longer my problem. The girls gave me their orders and I put them in the computer. The café is essentially more of a creperie. They serve crepes, salads and sandwiches, none of which are all that great. But it's always busy and people seem to love it. Since people in D.C. seem to settle for just about anything, this place is considered borderline amazing. One of the featured salads on the menu was a chicken salad, with mushrooms and gruyere-cheese served warm. Two of the ladies at the table ordered it and when I returned with their meals, the girl with long frizzy hair gave me a face that looked like I was serving her a dead baby on a plate.

"What the hell is this?" she asked as I put her chicken salad in front of her.

"It's a chicken salad, isn't that what you ordered?" I replied.

"Yes, but the chicken is all chopped up," she said. Who were these people?

"The chicken comes chopped up. Does it make a difference?" I replied.

"Well, usually, when you order a salad that has chicken on it, they serve it as a breast of chicken and you chop it up yourself."

"We have just cut out the middle man for you here," I said as if I had done her an enormous favor.

"Did this chicken come from a can?" she asked.

"Excuse me?" I looked at her with confusion in my eyes.

"Did this chicken come from a can?" she asked again.

Not once in my twenty-five years had I ever seen chicken come from a can. I really did not know that this was a culinary possibility.

"Does chicken come from a can?" I asked. I was being serious with her. "If it does, I have certainly never seen it before and certainly not in this restaurant."

I looked at her in the eyes. I could tell she had nothing to come back at me with. I really thought that we were heading toward a chicken of the sea conversation and kind of felt bad for her stupidity. She opted not to go there and instead asked to see the menu again.

"Your friend does not seem to mind the fact that her chicken came chopped up." I said referring to the only girl at the table who had not pissed me off and ordered the exact same thing as the girl who was complaining.

"Yea, this is good," the third girl said, scarffing down the salad.

"I can't eat this," the frizzy haired girl said. "I hate chopped up chicken!"

"Were you planning on eating a whole breast of chicken in one bite?" I asked. Now I was getting angry. Other tables needed me and these bitches were pissing me off with their ridiculous demands.

"No. I just don't like chopped up chicken and you should have told me that this salad was not served with a whole breast of chicken."

Jesus Christ! I had every intention of stabbing this girl in the heart with a steak knife, but there wasn't one around. Perhaps, a butter knife would have done the trick. As I was plotting this girl's death, the Russian girl chimed in again:

"Oh my God, what is this?" she screamed. I thought that she may have found a hair or something in her food, which at this place was just about an everyday occurrence. I looked at her plate and saw nothing but a runny egg.

"This egg is runny!" the Russian screamed.

I took the menu out of the frizzy haired girls hand and shoved it in the Russians face.

"Look!" I yelled pointing to what she ordered on the menu. "This is what you ordered." I shoved the menu in her face. "Your crepe comes with an egg over easy! In America, an over easy egg is usually runny." I took the menu and threw it on the ground. "What do you want?" I screamed at the frizzy haired girl. She ordered something else and I picked up the chicken salad and flung it in on the bar. I turned to the quiet girl and yelled, "while we are at it do *you* have anything to complain about or did you friends do enough complaining for the three of you?" She looked at me as if she was a puppy and I had just kicked her. She nodded "no" and I put the bitchy girl's new order into the computer. I hated waiting on people but these girls took annoying the shit out of me to a whole new level. After the bitchy girls order came, they ate quickly and left. I turned my attention to the two gay guys who were sitting next to them who I had pretty much ignored while trying to deal with the Great Chicken Debacle of 2008.

"Maybe those girls were so bitchy because their hair was unmanageable," one of the gay guys said. Nothing like a few bitchy queens to make a girl feel better.

"Were they awful or was it just me?" I asked.

"They were horrible!" the other gay said, "all they did was bitch about everything. They even took their bitching beyond today and started bitching about the service at the restaurant they had gone to last night."

"Jesus. I am so glad I don't date girls!" I said.

"Cheers to that!" they said as they clinked their champagne glasses together.

"You know, I am in AA now," I told the two of them as if we had been lifelong friends. They looked at me with confusion in their eyes and I walked away. Had this been the previous Sunday, I would have poured myself a glass of champagne, joined them and talked about how much I hated everyone. But this was the new Mark, so I would have to take my anger out by smoking a ridiculous amount of cigarettes and possibly eating a whole cake when I got home. I realized that these girls where just bitches and I was not really their problem. They just sucked at life and I happened to be in their line of fire that day.

I left the café that day feeling defeated. People annoyed me so much that I felt I was going to have to go into seclusion in order to stop drinking. What I really needed to do was learn how to deal with people and not make a huge production out of it. This task seemed daunting and I did not know if I was up for the challenge. As the day was coming to an end, I realized that the next day would be one week of sobriety. I had made it through the weekend, dealing with nervous breakdowns over chopped chicken and everyone I knew going out and drinking without drinking myself. Perhaps, I could do this after all. That evening Dr. Jake called after having returned from his trip to New York.

"How was it?" I asked.

"So much fun!" he replied. Already a pang of jealousy came over me. I felt he was partially responsible for my uncontrollable drinking over the summer and it simply was not fair for him to be having fun when I was completely miserable. "I saw *Equus* on Broadway," he continued. There was a Broadway revival of *Equus* going on at the time and the guy who played Harry Potter went full frontal at the end of it.

"You just liked it because you got to see Harry Potter's penis, you pervert!"

"Not true. It was an excellent play." For someone who thought *Mamma Mia!* was high art, I was not really buying this at all.

"Whatever."

"How was your weekend?" he asked.

"The usual, I was at the café all weekend, annoyed."

"That sucks. When am I going to be able to see you again?" Dr. Jake asked in his needy, pathetic voice.

"Maybe sometime this week," I replied. "Did you sleep with anyone while you were in New York?"

"No."

"Good. I have to go."

It seemed as if I was doing a really good job of keeping him in check while I was recovering. I went to bed that day feeling pretty good. Even though this weekend was a shit show, I didn't drink.

DAY TEN

What a fucked up dream I had last night. I was sitting on a beach drinking Bloody Marys with Bunny McDougall from AA. It was a lovely day. They sun was shining bright and the water was just perfect. Bunny and I had found just the perfect spot on the beach, away from all of the children. Bunny and I sat and enjoyed the sun. Well, I enjoyed the sun. Bunny was sitting quite nicely under a huge umbrella with a huge sun hat on. Her face already looked like a leather handbag so I assumed she was not trying to make it any worse. After a few minutes, Buns opened the cooler that we had brought with us. Hoping she was going to pull out sandwiches, because I am a fat ass, I was shocked to find she pulled out a bottle of Ketel One and Bloody Mary mix.

"I made the mix myself," Bunny said.

"Wait a second, we can't drink Bloody Marys, we're in AA," I said.

"Oh don't worry about it. I won't tell if you won't." So this is what she and Palmer Courtlandt were doing with their spare time. "I have been doing this for years, dear. Just have one, no one will know." She poured a Bloody and handed it to me. It was so hot and I was really thirsty. I took the drink in my hand and knocked it back. For the rest of the afternoon Buns and I drank all we wanted and didn't get drunk.

"SHIT!" I yelled upon waking up. I took my pillow and tried to hide it under my blanket as if it was a bottle of vodka. After a minute, I realized it was just a dream. "Thank God" I thought. I did not stay sober for ten days just to fuck it up now. But what did all of this mean? I had done such a great job of not drinking my brain was confused. I needed to get to the bottom of this.

I was the first person in the AA meeting that day. This had never happened before. I was so freaked out by the dream I had, I wanted to make sure I was on sacred ground so I would not actually take a drink. The funny thing was, I really did not want to drink. After a few days of waiting on tables filled with drunks, drinking had lost its appeal on me. All I could think about was how shitty all of the people who were drinking were going to feel in the morning and I never wanted to feel hung-over ever again. So why was I having this dream? As I sat and waited for the rest of the group to come in, I took a look at what was around me at the AA clubhouse. The paint on the walls was a lovely baby throw up green. In the center of the far side of the wall, there was a fireplace. I assumed that it did not work as one of the crazier alcoholics may have attempted to light themselves on fire at one point. All along the walls there were framed pieces of paper that had sayings such as "Let Go and Let God" and *One Day at A Time*. Having been in AA long enough, I knew that these signs were not advertisements for the amazing 70's sitcom starring Bonnie Franklin, but AA sayings that were supposed to help. I was so worried about myself that I hadn't even taken the time to look around and see my surroundings. I saw the plants on the mantle that the secretary of the meeting was always telling everyone not to water. I had only been in AA for ten days, but every day there was a reminder not to water the plants. I wondered why people needed to be reminded of such things every single day, but those alcoholics have been known to be a crazy plant-watering bunch. It was about five minutes before anyone walked in. The first person I saw walk through the door was Laura Lesbian. *Thank God,* I thought. I could definitely talk to her.

Laura walked over and took a seat near me. "Hey Mark, what's going on?" she asked.

I turned to her and said, "Oh my God, I had the most fucked up dream last night."

"Oh yea, what was it?" she asked.

"I had a dream that I was drinking Bloody Marys on the beach with the fabulous older woman who always looks so dressed up."

"Bobbi?" Laura asked.

I still did not know what her name was, as I was still referring to her as Bunny McDougall. "I guess so. I have never even spoken to her before, but I did always think she would be fun to drink with. It was such a confusing dream. Why would we be drinking Bloody Marys? Don't you think margaritas or beers are more appropriate for the beach?"

She laughed. "Oh baby, you had your first drinking dream," she said.

"What?"

"Drinking dream. When you stop drinking, your mind will play some super fucked up games with you. I've been sober for a year and a half and I still have them. Don't worry, it's natural."

Great, so this is what I had to look forward to, dreaming every night about an eighty year-old woman whose name I didn't even know. We all sat down as the meeting began and I listened intently to the speaker. She was telling the group that once she began coming to AA meetings she realized that she needed to get rid of all of the people in her life that enabled her to drink. I thought about who I needed to get rid of in my life. At this point, it would have to be anyone I was friends with in D.C. because everyone I associated myself with drank quite a bit. I figured I would hold off on that because it had taken me so long to make friends to begin with, I didn't have the energy to make a whole new set of friends now. My family definitely made me want to drink, but I couldn't really get rid of them – we were pretty much stuck together until death. Then I thought of Dr. Jake. Everything he did pretty much made me want to drink. True, we were no longer "together", but all of the stresses of being in a relationship were still present. I was still dealing with all of his bullshit on a daily basis, but with none of the perks. We were no longer having sex because I was afraid if we had sex and he hurt my feelings, I would start drinking again. Instead of waiting until the very last minute, until both of our feelings were hurt beyond belief, I decided to take make a big girl decision and tell Dr. Jake that the only relationship we could have was a friendship. It was exciting to be making a true grown up decision. I called Dr. Jake after the meeting ended.

"Jake," I said into the phone.

"Hey Mark, what's going on?" he replied.

"Nothing, just got out of a meeting."

"How are the drunks today?" Jake said with a laugh.

I laughed as well. "Crazy as ever," I replied. "Listen, I need to talk to you about something. It's kind of hard for me to do this, but I feel it's necessary for my recovery." I was so dramatic when speaking of my "recovery," but Dr. Jake was used to it at this point.

"What is it?" he replied.

"I really don't think it is a good idea for us to continue whatever it is we have going on." I could hear defeat in his sigh. "I don't think we should be having sex and I also think that we should be moving on. It's not healthy for either one of us to continue like this." I could not believe the words were coming out of my mouth. I was notorious for dragging things on until the last possible minute.

"Does that mean we aren't having sex anymore ever?" he asked. For someone with two post-graduate degrees, Dr. Jake was a little slow on the uptake.

"Yes."

"Yes, we can or yes we can't."

"Jesus, Jake. No more sex."

"Oh," he said. "Well, I guess if this is what is going to help you, I have no choice."

"No, you really don't." He really should have seen this coming. Dr. Jake was like a sex addict. He wanted it all the time. I guess it had something to do with the fact that he was married to his ugly ass wife for so long. The only way he was going to be getting into my pants from now on was going to be involuntary, and God forbid it come to that. Jake, to my surprise, quickly changed conversation topics.

"I am thinking about going up to New York again this weekend for Halloween," he said. Damn him! He always knew just how to piss me off. No one deserved to go to New York except for me, and he knew this. Perhaps friendship was out of the question.

"Why? Weren't you just there?" I asked

"I had a good time and I have nothing else to do," he replied. He asked me where good places were to go out and told me that he would call me when he got back. I had made some pretty good suggestions and thought about last Halloween when I got totally loaded and made out with some kid who was in his pajamas. Those were the good old days. I was suspicious of why Dr. Jake was going back to New York so soon, but kept my suspicions to myself. After all, upon my request, we were no longer dating, or doing whatever it was that we were doing.

I went about my day as usual, going to the gym and then to work. I had a nice little routine going and was happy to be following it. The café was as obnoxious as usual that night, but a particular table kept holding me up. They were sitting around drinking and were my last table so I politely implied that it was time for me to go, therefore time for them to go as well. I was ready for bed, didn't these people understand that? Feeling that they were being rude by not taking the hint that I was ready to go, I threw their check on the table and told them to get out. It's nice to know that my bad attitude continued in sobriety. I would have expected nothing less.

DAY ELEVEN

When I first began going to AA, I had decided to dress up for the event, not knowing who I might run into. I've always been told to make a good first impression and what better way to do that than to dress fashionably. However, after a few days, I realized that I was the only one who felt that way, so I decided to drop that idea and wear my gym clothes to the meetings. No one else around me was dressed terribly well so I stopped caring. I also really did not know any of these people, so within the first few days I stopped wearing my Sunday Best. I did not think that anyone new was going to pop up so it was really not an issue, until I sat down that day next to a guy who must have been a model. I had no idea where he came from, but I was pretty sure I was in love with him at first sight. He was one of the most gorgeous guys I had ever laid my eyes on. He looked like one of those models that were always standing under a waterfall somewhere modeling a Calvin Klein fragrance. He was tall, with very dark long hair and light eyes. He was absolutely gorgeous and I sat throughout the meeting making my sexy *come and get me* faces at him. He did not seem to be paying much attention to me but within the hour, I had already planned our wedding and what our 2.5 alcoholic children would have looked like. As the meeting ended, I was tempted to walk over and introduce myself and ask him if he was interested in starting a life together. Unfortunately, I was interrupted by a balding twenty-something on my way over.

"Hey!" the balding gay kid said to me. "My name is Brett." He was clearly giving me the once over.

"I'm Mark," I responded. I tried to listen to what Brett had to say but could not pay attention. My eyes were following the handsome model as he was walking toward the door. Damn you Brett for ruining my love life! Who did this kid think he was? After all, this man was most likely to be my true love. The model walked out the door and I turned my attention to back to Brett who was rambling on about some gay AA meeting that took place down the street.

"It's a really great meeting," he said. "Sometimes afterwards, we go out for frozen yogurt or cupcakes." I tried to pay attention to what he had to say but his breath reeked of halitosis and I was really pissed that this kid had totally just cock blocked me at AA.

"Whatever," I said. "Call me when you guys start going to Happy Hour after the meetings." No one cock blocks Mark Rosenberg. I turned and walked out the door looking for my hot model as I turned each corner down the street.

Suddenly, I had a renewed interest in AA. Tomorrow, I was going to have to come looking my absolute best.

DAY TWELVE

I came to AA that day looking like a million bucks. After almost two weeks of not drinking, I had pretty much lost my beer belly. Pair that with the fact that I had been working out like a maniac, I was beginning to look less like a bloated Alpine and more like how a respectable gay man was supposed to look - a gym rat. Today I was wearing an outfit designed by Diesel (especially designed for me, if the hot model were to ask). I had on a tight long sleeved shirt and an even tighter pair of jeans to show off what little ass I had. As I walked in, I saw my model and made a beeline to sit next to him. No one but me was getting their claws into this one.

The meeting began, as it always did and the leader of the group did his usual shtick. I was still relatively new to the meetings, but whoever the speaker was pretty much said the same thing. They were a drunk and now they aren't thanks to AA. Pretty standard. After the speaker finished, the meeting was open and my hot model boyfriend raised his hand to speak.

"My name is Victor, and I'm an alcoholic," he said. I thought his name was perfect. We could name our first daughter Victoria, just like on *One Life to Live*. Victor went on to tell his story. He revealed that he was, in fact, a model many years ago for a very recognizable brand. I suspected Calvin Klein, but you never know. There were always a lot of sad models standing under waterfalls for Gucci as well. While modeling, Victor would be invited to parties where the booze was abundant. He began drinking regularly until it became a problem and he soon found himself smoking crack out of a Coke can under the Brooklyn Bridge.

Yes! Now we are getting down to the real shit. This is what I wanted to hear. Victor concluded by telling everyone that he finally had hit rock bottom and came to AA, where he has been for the past four years. He, like everyone else around me, was grateful for what AA had done for him. He had come from the very bottom and was now healthy and successful again. His story was inspiring. If he could stop drinking and smoking crack out of Coke cans surely, I could make a better life for myself.

As the meeting continued, I decided that mine and Victor's second child would be named Bo, if it were a boy and Tina if it was a girl. After the meeting, I mustered up enough courage to will myself to speak to him, but people bombarded him. Everyone was interested in him. And I had some stiff competition. Palmer Courtlandt was eye fucking the shit out him during the whole meeting. As people surrounded Victor, I saw out of the corner of my eye that Brett was approaching. Damn him and his awful breath and cup cake chatter. He had already foiled my plot to speak to Victor yesterday, and I was not about to have him do it again. I slipped into the bathroom, giving him the, *I am about to shit my pants look* and waited there for about five minutes, until I figured Brett would have left. But when I came out of the bathroom, Victor had gone. That was the last time I ever saw him. People that beautiful don't live in D.C. and I should have known better. He had probably been whisked away to Milan shortly after the meeting ended. I would have to put hopes of meeting my future baby's daddy on the back burner.

As I was leaving the meeting, a friendly looking guy walked up toward me.

"Hi, I'm Luke," he said, sticking out his hand and I shook it. "You're new here?"

What did I have a fucking sign on my back or something?

"Yes," I replied.

"Here," he said as he took out a card from his briefcase and handed it to me. "Take my card and call me if you need anything." I took his card and he walked away. He was pretty cute, and always being on the lookout for ass, I took his card and put it in my pocket. However, I did not know at the time that taking his card was going to be the smartest thing I had done in sobriety, because he was going to be there for some of the hardest times in my life.

I had decided to attempt to be a nicer person in sobriety. Surely, I had not gotten sober to be miserable and make everyone's life around me a living hell. I was beginning to listen more when people around me were speaking and would even respond with helpful hints.

"I really need to get a new sling for my apartment," a friend would ask.

"Try the Leather Rack," I would respond, Google mapping it on my phone.

Sobriety also helped me focus more and one thing I was definitely focusing on was keeping in good shape. After all, no one likes a fatty. Especially one who spends his afternoons with a bunch of alcoholics.

I arrived at the gym that afternoon, feeling all right. Maybe Victor was not my future husband after all, but I was going to work out and forget about all that. I walked into the locker room and found that I was the only one in there, except for an older man who was changing. I walked over to my locker, put my bag down and began to change. The older man walked over to me. I hate making conversation with old men at the gym. It's like they don't even work out; they just sit and the locker room and wait for someone to talk to. I decided I would be nice to the elderly gentleman.

"Did you play sports in high school?" the old man asked. I had hoped that this conversation was not going to turn into a sexual fantasy for him later.

"I ran track briefly," I said. "I was subsequently kicked off the team after I started smoking."

"That's nice. I played football in college."

"Oh," I replied, putting my sneakers on. I was changing at warp speed, but he was still rambling on.

"I remember the first time we all had to shower together after a football game," he continued. I think he must have played football before the birth of the NFL. But I decided that the new, nice Mark was not going to comment. "I remember standing under the water in the shower and it was very cold. All of the sudden, I felt a warm sensation on my chest." I did not like where this story was heading. "Then, I looked up and saw that the quarterback was peeing on my chest."

"That's revolting!" I said.

"It was kind of like initiation," he said. "But, I kind of liked it."

Ew, I thought. This was turning into really low budget porn.

"Do you want to pee on me?" the old man said. I lost it. I could not be nice anymore. This man was filthy and I could no longer be cordial.

"WHAT THE FUCK ARE YOU TALKING ABOUT YOU SICK SON OF A BITCH?" I yelled as I grabbed my things and ran out of the locker room. So much for trying to be a nicer person.

I really hate D.C. Everyone is such a mess here.

DAY FIFTEEN

The next few days passed uneventfully. I was beginning to get into the swing of things and living my life without drinking. But one thing was bothering me. Many people in the meetings told me that I needed to get rid of the people I used to drink with because they could turn out to be bad influences in my life. As it turned out, people had stopped calling me anyway. I had told everyone that I would be able to go out and socialize without drinking, but no one seemed to believe me. To prove it, I surprised a group of friends who I knew were going out and met up with them.

Everyone seemed to be happy to see me, but everyone seemed to be walking on eggshells around me. It did not bother me that everyone else was drinking and I wasn't, but it seemed to make everyone around me uncomfortable. I walked up to one of my friends who I had not seen in a few weeks and we chatted. When a friend of his that I had not met came up, my friend introduced me to the stranger.

"This is Mark, my friend I was telling you about," my friend said, "He does not drink anymore, but, don't worry; we'll have him back soon!"

On that note, I left the bar. How could my so-called friends be willing me to fail at my latest venture? These were people I had been through so much with. I simply could not believe that our friendship hinged on whether or not I drank. Maybe the AAs were right. Maybe I could not associate myself with these people any longer. Maybe they were not good people for me to be hanging out with anymore.

I went home and felt defeated. I felt like everyone around me was trying to make me fail. When Erica Kane went to rehab on *All My Children*, everyone was there to help her. Even her cokehead brother Mark made a cameo to show his support. But no one was really supporting me and I was beginning to feel more and more alone. As I got ready for bed, I went on facebook to see what was going on with everyone. Facebook is great for keeping up with people who you have not seen in a long time and reconnecting you with former schoolmates. However, it can also remind you why you don't keep in touch with certain people anymore. I had gone to Dr. Jake's page to see what he was doing. It said that he was currently in New York. This, of course, pissed me off even more. Everyone was having fun but me. I threw myself a small pity party and ended up going to bed very angry that evening.

DAY SIXTEEN

I went to AA today and was trying to erase the memory of the previous nights' events. I bumped into Laura Lesbian and she told me that she had faced many of the same problems that I was facing right now. She told me to just hang on and that things would eventually work themselves out. After all it was God's way.

One thing that I was not really grasping in AA was the whole God thing. I was never a very religious person and was not sure that I could grasp the whole concept that everything was God's plan. After all, I am Jewish, and don't my people believe in self-pity and butting into other people's business?

After the meeting, I went home and felt very lonely. I felt as if I had no friends and everyone was against me. I had tried to put forth a positive attitude, but it seemed that I could not will myself to feel any better. That evening, I decided to call Luke, the guy who gave me his number a few days before.

"Hey, I am glad you called," Luke said into the phone.

"Oh, thanks. I was just calling to say 'hi'," I said. "I am feeling a bit like I have no friends in the world."

"It's OK, I felt that way the first few months of sobriety as well, but, as they as they say, this too shall pass." There was that God business again.

"Whatever." I was hoping to just ignore this God nonsense for as long as possible. "It's weird because I am feeling great physically, but mentally I am a freaking mess," I said.

"Yea, I remember when I first stopped drinking. I went to a therapist who basically told me that I was crazier than a shit house rat," he laughed. "But, we all are, and as long as you don't drink, today will be a good day."

I wondered if it would. Some of my best days had been drinking days. Maybe it was time to change my attitude a bit.

"I guess," I replied. "But, I work in a bar and I cannot seem to find another job. Everyone I know drinks and I feel like I am constantly missing out on things."

"First of all, you can stay sober anywhere. My first few months of sobriety, I worked in a bar and I was just fine. Secondly, you are not missing out on anything; you are living your life with a clear head. You no longer wake up hung-over and you can get things done and try to have a positive outlook on life." Easier said than done. "Listen, tomorrow is my one-year anniversary of sobriety, are you going to be at the meeting? We are having cake and coffee afterwards."

"Well, if you are having cake, then I am totally there," I said. He laughed, thinking I was joking, not knowing what I huge fan of free cake I am.

"Ok, then I will see you tomorrow."

He hung up. I went to bed that night and had the most fabulous dream about getting blackout drunk on flirtinis with Luke and Palmer Courtlandt.

DAY SEVENTEEN

"I am so happy to have my best friend back!" Tom yelled into the phone that morning. "This is the best thing that you have ever done. Now all you have to do is get your ass back to New York so we can take this town by storm again!" Tom and I had, at one point, done quite a bit of drinking and drugging together. However, Tom eventually settled down and I began drinking for the both of us. All of the problems that we had with our friendship were due to my drinking and Tom was still the only person with enough balls to tell me that I needed to go to AA. "Say it!" Tom then said into the phone. "Say what I know you are thinking right now."

I sighed into the phone and replied, "You were right!"

"Again. I am right again. I am always right fuckface, and don't you forget it!" he laughed. "So what are you doing today?"

"I am going to steal some pens from the bank and then head to a meeting. You know you have to go every day?" I said. We continued to chat for a few more minutes. I was so happy that Tom and I were speaking again. We had had a falling out a few months before when I had accidentally almost killed his dogs after leaving cocaine out in his apartment. This was not the first time this had happened and somehow, Tom managed to continue to speak to me, even though I was a walking disaster. I really believe that Tom knew that most of the shenanigans I pulled were because I was usually drunk and would overreact about things because of it. I was glad to be back in Tom's inner circle and was feeling a bit better as I walked in to the AA meeting that day.

That day I was feeling super nostalgic, and rolled into the AA meeting rocking out to UB40's "Red, Red Wine" and quickly realized that that was blatantly inappropriate. When I arrived, I saw that Luke was in the leader's chair. It was his one-year anniversary of sobriety and he was going to share his experience with the group. Behind him, I saw a fabulous looking chocolate cake with vanilla icing, with my name on it. Actually, Luke's name was on it, but I could totally see my face in it within the next hour. I opted not to think about cake and instead listen to Luke's story.

Luke began and told everyone that he was originally from Oklahoma and came to D.C. for school. As soon as he was free from his family's crutches, he took up drinking and continued to drink just about every day for the next ten years. He had reached bottom several times, but continued to drink even when he knew he shouldn't. He had lost friends because of it, but physically could not bring himself to stop drinking until he came to AA. I thought, once again, that Luke and I had the same story. I learned after a few weeks in AA that we all have the same story, just as Laura Lesbian told me on my second day. But something about what Luke said drew me to him. He physically could not stop drinking alone. I had felt the same way, before I came to AA. He had lost friends because of his drinking. Tom and I had drifted apart for some time because my drinking had gotten out of control. I was not being honest with myself for the longest time about anything and now, I was beginning to awaken to the fact that I had been wrong in the past and that I did have a problem. After Luke finished speaking, I leapt to my feet with applause. Everyone around me looked at me like I was an asshole. Eventually everyone ended up standing with me and clapping for Luke. I felt as if I had known him my whole life.

After the meeting was over, Luke introduced me to his boyfriend Franklin, a good-looking Asian guy who was sitting in the meeting. Luke explained that Franklin was not an alcoholic, but came to celebrate Luke's anniversary date. Luke and I were alike in just about every way, except, I really don't have a thing for Asian guys. We definitely differ there. We all got to know each other a little better and ate cake.

"We should have cake every meeting," I said with icing around my mouth. "I think it would make people a little more willing to show up. You know, it's like incentive for not drinking." Everyone laughed at what a pig I was but I was not joking. I love cake and could talk about it for hours. We all ended up going our separate ways. Before we left, Luke told me to call him this weekend so that we could chat. I was so happy that I had found a new friend that I went to the bakery down the street and got a whole cake to eat by myself in celebration of seventeen days of not drinking.

DAY TWENTY

"Hey Mark, how's it going?" Dr. Jake said into the phone. I know I had told Dr. Jake that I wanted to stay friends with him, but I didn't really mean it. He pissed me off and the fact that he did not have to go to AA aggravated me even more.

"Nothing much, just getting along. You?" I asked.

"I am OK. I am actually calling to ask you for a favor."

"What is it?"

"Well, I am going to come out to my parents and I wanted to see if you had any pointers on it." He had already, at this point, told his parents that he was getting a divorce from his wife over the summer. Now, I suppose he felt it was time for him to bust open the closet doors and tell his family he was gay. I didn't really see the need for him to do this because as far as I was concerned, Dr. Jake was living in a glass closet anyway.

"I don't know what you want me to tell you," I said. I had been dealing with sobriety and my own problems and I really did not have any pearls of wisdom to share with him.

"You know that our time together was very special to me. That's why I am asking you for help," he said in a very shaky voice. I figured something was up.

"What were you doing in New York?" I questioned, changing topics abruptly.

"Do you really want to know?" he asked.

"Well, if you did not want me to know, then you would have not posted on facebook that you were in New York, would you?" Check and mate.

"I am seeing someone in New York."

I paused. How in twenty days had Dr. Jake managed to find a boyfriend? I don't mean to toot my own horn or anything, but I am so much better looking than him. I also do not have the baggage of an estranged wife and the Army hanging over me. Just alcoholism.

"What?" I asked.

"I knew I should not have told you. I did not mean to hurt your feelings, but it just happened. I thought you had moved on anyway. Your facebook status said that you just got busy in a Burger King bathroom"

"Those are lyrics from the Humpty Hump song you fucking moron," I paused. "So let me get this straight." I cleared my throat, in anticipation of bombarding him with insults. Then I remembered a previous conversation, a few weeks back, when Dr. Jake asked me where to go out in New York. "So you not only asked me where to take your new boyfriend out in New York, but now you are asking me for help coming out to your parents. Are you fucking kidding me right now?"

"It's just...I don't...I..."

"You're a fucking douche bag, Jake. I cannot believe that you are doing this right now. You know I need as little stress in my life as possible and you are just one constant source of it."

"But, I need your help."

"Why don't you ask your new boyfriend for help, you horses ass!"

"It's just you mean so much to me...I..."

"Fuck you. If I meant anything to you, we would not be having this conversation right now. You are so inconsiderate. It's almost as if you want me to get drunk and come crawling back to you."

There it was. The truth. There was no way he could hide from it now. Dr. Jake was such a mess that he needed someone to be as big of a mess as he was to make himself feel better. I was no longer a possible candidate for the position. I could see now what Dr. Jake was doing and I could no longer be a party to it. I was not going to be his punching bag anymore. Dr. Jake continued on until finally I interrupted him.

"Listen you son of a bitch, if I hear from you ever again, I am going to come to your house with a baseball bat and beat the living shit out of you!" I screamed into the phone and hung up. He should have known that was an idle threat as I have never once played baseball in my life nor have I ever owned a baseball bat.

I was pacing in my living room, not knowing what to do. I wanted a drink so badly but knew that's exactly what Dr. Jake would have wanted.

He wanted me to drink and lose this battle I was fighting against my demons. Instead, I chain smoked a few cigarettes and continued pacing. After a few moments, I realized that I had strength that I had not had before. I was like Gloria Estefan – I was coming out of the dark. My feelings for him were gone so what difference did it make? Had this conversation taken place a few weeks ago, I would have opened a bottle and began a drinking binge that would have lasted for days. But I was not going to be Blair Cramer any longer! Blair Cramer is a character on *One Life to Live* who always went back to her husband Todd, even after he raped someone, killed someone, almost raped someone again, stole Blair's baby and made her think it was dead, almost kidnapped his own daughter's baby, was raped himself and pretended to have multiple personalities. No matter what, Blair always went back to Todd. I was not going to be Blair any longer. I was going to be strong, like her Aunt Dorian. She didn't put up with shit from anyone. I was not going to let someone else's actions make me weaken. I was strong now. I could take down an entire corporation if need be.

I realized that I needed a break from all of the nonsense going on in D.C. An impromptu trip was just what the doctor ordered.

DAY TWENTY-ONE

"With the taste of your lips, I'm on a ride...Your toxic I'm slippin' under!" The radio was blasting Britney Spears and the windows were rolled down as my brother and I were driving down the expressway with the lights of Atlantic City upon us.

"What better way to celebrate twenty one days sober than a trip to Atlantic City?" I said as we pulled up to Caesar's Palace.

"I really don't know," my brother, Kevin said as he pulled the car into a parking spot. "I am so excited. I love gambling! This was a great idea!"

"I know, sobriety has filled me such great ideas. Next month we should hit up Monte Carlo," I said. "I needed to get out of D.C. I don't even care if I win money or not. If nothing else, we will put some money into the New Jersey economy so they can fix the hole in the ozone that's directly above this state. Jersey girls do love their hairspray!"

We walked into Caesar's with dreams of winning big. I love Atlantic City because of its gaudiness. It's amazing to me that so many people think spandex and teased hair is still fashionable and that they all convene in one place. I also love Atlantic City because you can smoke just about anywhere. The night that my brother and I were in town, was the night of the Madonna concert so the casinos were filled with gay men. It was like a gay wet dream. What more could a homo ask for?

I usually have terrible luck in life, except when it comes to gambling. I don't know how it happened, but a few months beforehand, I won about a thousand dollars playing roulette. I really didn't know what I was doing, but just ended up putting down money on a few numbers and won a bunch back. I had hoped that lightning would strike twice as I sat down at the roulette tables again.

"Hi Nancy," I said to the woman spinning the roulette wheel, as if we had been life long friends. I put my money down and lost. I tried again but lost. After about sixteen times of flat out losing money, I told my brother that I was going to play penny slots with the old ladies and to find me there if he needed me.

I sat down next to a row of old ladies putting coins into machines with cigarettes hanging out of their mouths. I always had dreams of turning into a slot junkie when I got older, but maybe now was the time. I could live in Atlantic City and just become a professional gambler. Think of the glamour of it all. As I sat and put my coins into the machines, I looked at my phone and noticed several texts had come in from Dr. Jake. Normally, I would have read each one and let whatever he had to say bother me, but instead, I deleted them. I put my last dollar into the machine and didn't win anything back. My luck had run out in Atlantic City and with Dr. Jake. I sat at the slot machine, smoking a cigarette and realized I had no use for Dr. Jake in my life anymore. I had no feelings for him and he was not adding anything to my life except aggravation. I was no longer interested in shedding tears for affairs that I no longer wanted anything to do with.

My brother and I returned to D.C. that night having lost about a thousand dollars between the two of us. I didn't really care. I needed to get away and do something a little crazy, and it felt good to do something out of the norm without drinking. I spent the car ride home wondering whether or not I could write this excursion off on my tax return.

DAY TWENTY-TWO

"I went to Atlantic City yesterday and lost a shit ton of money," I said to Luke as we were eating lunch. "Pretty dumb idea, huh?"

"At least you didn't drink," he replied.

"I would have probably lost a lot less money had I been drinking," I said.

"But you didn't."

"Whatever."

"I am glad, that with everything that happened with Jake, you did not revert back to your old ways."

"Thanks!" I said. Luke and I had become fast friends and I really liked having lunch and going to meetings with him.

"I think I should be your sponsor," he said. After nearly a month in AA, I still had not had a sponsor. In AA, sponsor is someone who guides you through the twelve steps. At this point, I had really not found anyone I was comfortable enough with to share everything that had gone on in my past. I liked Luke and he didn't judge me. I thought it would be a good idea to have him sponsor me.

"That would be awesome," I said.

"Great. The first thing I want you to do is make a list of how your life became unmanageable because of alcohol and the things that led up to you coming to AA. Think back and bring your list to me within the next few days."

This task seemed rather daunting, but at this point, I really wanted to make this AA thing work. That night, I went home and made a list of how alcohol had made my life unmanageable. It was rather long.

How Alcohol Made My Life Unmanageable:

1. Freshman year of college, I got drunk and watched Britney Spears' world tour and tried to learn the choreography to every dance instead of doing a term paper.

2. Forgot to return *Little Shop of Horrors* to Blockbuster and never paid the $88 late fee, instead spending that money on booze. Banned from Blockbuster for life.

3. Got drunk at my brother's Bar Mitzvah rehearsal. Was not allowed to be in my brother's Bar Mitzvah.

4. Once ate a homeless man's sandwich.

5. Got drunk waiting tables at a restaurant in New York and drank a

glass of wine that was sitting on a woman's table that she paid for, then lied about it, while she was sitting right there and saw me do it.

6. Got drunk and promised my niece I would give her a horse. She is still waiting for it.

7. Passed out in a stranger's apartment in Atlanta and did not know whose apartment I was in or how to get back to my hotel.

8. Let a fat guy give me a hand job in the bathroom of a club while blacked out.

9. Ruined a white jacket when I was blacked out and making out with a guy against a wall that had just been painted.

10. Got kicked out of a club in New York for getting drunk and stealing the velvet rope.

The list went on and on. I could not believe that I remembered half of the things that were on it. As I read the list, I finally realized that my life had become unmanageable because of alcohol. Normal people did not get into the kind of trouble that I found myself getting into on a weekly basis. It was then I realized that I was doing the right thing for myself. I made a decision and I needed to have courage in my convictions. I felt that I now had the strength to do this and I was going to make good things happen for myself.

DAY TWENTY-FOUR

I made a wrong turn and ended up going into a Narcotics Anonymous meeting today. I didn't even realize I had done it until everyone started talking about shooting heroin. I was too embarrassed to leave in the middle of it, so I stayed and listened. I thought I had it bad. How wrong I was.

DAY TWENTY-FIVE

Life finally seemed to be moving in the right direction for me. I felt myself becoming a happier person and looking at things and seeing the glass half full. I was making sober friends, and still trying to keep in contact with my not-so-sober friends. I was living a healthy lifestyle and smoking more cigarettes than I ever thought possible.

I really appreciated having Luke's friendship and we continued to bond. That day in AA, after days of paying attention to what everyone was saying, I began to drift off. I may have been sober but I was as A.D.D. as ever. I thought it was time that the members of my AA meeting put on a talent show. Better yet, we could do on a full on production. Something everyone likes like *Bye, Bye Birdie*. Little orphan Annie would totally kill playing Kim McAfee. The thought passed and I refocused my attention.

I began to like my routine and I was beginning to like AA. Even the cafe had gotten better. That night a group of fifteen Asian girls came in and sat in my section, taking up most of it.

"Can I get you guys anything to drink?" I asked.

"Water," the first girl said.

"Water," the second girl said.

"Water," the third girl said.

"Water."

"Water."

"Water."

DAMN IT! ONE OF YOU NEEDS TO ORDER A FUCKING DRINK SO I CAN MAKE SOME MONEY!!! I was thinking evil thoughts but instead of voicing them, I kept them to myself. Progress. Asian girls are notorious for not ordering anything in restaurants and sitting all night sipping water or tea. I got the fifteen girls their water and returned to find that not only were they only drinking water, but they would also be splitting food. Fifteen girls, drinking water, ordering three things and taking up my whole section on a Saturday night. Normally, I would have kicked them out, and yelled something racist at them, but instead, I let them stay there for a while and politely asked them to leave when they were finished because I had a table that was going to eat dinner. They got up and left and no one was killed. Small victories.

DAY THIRTY

Finally, I get my first chip! I was so excited about today. I had made it a full month without drinking and it was not nearly as miserable as I thought it would be. I went to AA that day and I received my first chip to applause and hugs. Shortly after I got out of the meeting, I received a call from Dr. Jake. He had been calling and texting me for several days and I had not answered, so I decided to see what he wanted.

"Mark, I need to tell you something," he said.

I thought he must have an STD or something awful that he had now given me.

"What is it?" I asked.

He paused and said, "I am still in love with you."

"No, you are not," I said.

"I am."

"No, Jake, you are not. You need to get over this and move on." I could not believe that the words were coming out of my mouth. I was acting more like a Dorian and less like a Blair every day. He continued to talk for a while and I let him go. I have not spoken to him since.

That night after I left work at the cafe, I saw that my friend, who worked at the bar next door, was having a birthday party and I went over to celebrate with her for a while.

"Mark!" she said as I entered. She had clearly been drinking, but was genuinely excited to see me nonetheless. We sat around and chatted and at midnight she had a champagne toast to celebrate her birthday. She raised her glass and put it to her lips then took the glass and put it in my face.

"Just have a sip Mark, no one will know." I smelled the champagne and thought how nice it would have been to take a sip of it. I then remembered everything that had led up to me going to AA in the first place. Knowing me, a sip of champagne would have lead to a case of champagne and I was feeling better than ever and not willing to give that up. I suddenly had self-control, something I had never had before.

"I will know," I responded and walked out the door. I walked home and thought about everything that had happened in the past month. It had been a long and emotional journey, but I had made it through a whole month of sobriety. I felt great and was ready to conquer anything that lay ahead. I had not changed myself, but I had changed my outlook on life. I was still the same person I always had been, I just wasn't drinking any longer. I had the strength to refrain from drinking and that was reason enough for me to continue to move forward sober, and stronger than ever.

BABY DADDY

A lot can happen in nine months. The first nine months of my sobriety was a blur. I had finally moved from Washington D.C. back to New York and moved from yelling at Asian girls at the café to yelling at Asian tourists who were looking for tickets to *Mamma Mia!* at my new job. Between meetings and making new friends, I felt I had inadvertently forgotten some of my old drinking buddies. These were people I had spent a good deal of time with and always had a fabulous story or two to tell. One of those friends was a colorful straight man who went by the name, Dane. We worked together at the café, and used to get completely trashed together just about every night. On a trip back to D.C. for a visit, I gave Dane a call and asked him if he would like to meet for lunch at our old favorite Mexican restaurant. He accepted my invite.

I sat and waited for Dane for what felt like hours. He was never on time for anything and today was no exception. While I sat, drinking my iced tea, Dane rolled into the restaurant like a whirling dervish. He plopped down at my table and we exchanged pleasantries.

"So what's been going on Dane?" I asked.

"Same shit!" Dane responded. As Dane was getting himself together, the waiter approached and asked:

"Can I get you something to – ."

"Margarita," Dane said, interrupting the waiter, "rocks, no salt."

"I see nothing has changed with you," I said with a laugh.

"Nope," he replied.

Dane and I sat and laughed for hours. I had forgotten that straight people can be really hilarious sometimes. Dane just had a way with words that was unbounded. I had never met anyone like him before. He was well spoken, even after he had downed two and half pitchers of margaritas and always had a ridiculous story to tell.

"What ever happened to Alexandra?" I asked, referring to a girl that Dane and I had gotten wasted with on several occasions. "She was such a fun girl."

"Oh, I didn't tell you?" he replied.

"Tell me what?" I asked.

"I am going to need another drink for this story." Dane flagged down the waiter and after he got another drink, he leaned toward and whispered, "If you tell anyone about this I will kill you."

"Uh, ok," I said. This had to be a whopper of a story.

"Well, remember the last night that you drank? The Miss Adams Morgan Day party?" I nodded, even though I only had a vague recollection of said event. "Afterwards, Alex and I went back to my place and fucked."

"Really?" I asked. Alexandra was totally out of Dane's league so this revelation was quite a surprise.

"Yes, and it was really good until the next morning. When we woke up, Alex threw up all over the place and got her period. It was really weird. I wanted to take care of her, but I wasn't feeling that great myself so I wasn't much help." As Dane continued his story, his hands, which were wrapped around his margarita glass were beginning to tremble.

"That is never a good way to wake up, especially with someone else is your bed."

"I know, it was frightening. She was like, violently ill," he continued, "but, I didn't think anything of it. When I called her a few weeks later, she told me that she had moved to Guatemala."

"That's weird, I thought she was Jewish." I asked not knowing why any Jew would want to move to Guatemala. I mean, we may have wondered that desert for forty years, but we really don't keep well in heat like that. Especially Jews with frizzy hair.

"I know, apparently, she had some extended family or something down there. Anyway, when I finally did get in touch with her, she told me that she was pregnant."

"Holy Shit!" I replied. Apparently, Dane's life had turned into *One Life to Live* in the time I hadn't seen him.

"Yea, I know," he said as he sipped his margarita. "Anyway, she didn't know if it was mine or not because she had been hooking up with another guy at the same time."

"Why didn't you just take a paternity test?" I asked.

"You can do that when the baby isn't born yet?"

"I don't fucking know, what do I look like a gynecologist? They do it on TV all the time though." At least they do on *One Life to Live* and that's as close to real life as it gets as far as I am concerned.

"Whatever," he continued, "so I was flipping out. I mean, I am really not ready to become a father. But then, after I thought about it, maybe I was." He wasn't. The man was like a hippie. Well, more like a hipster. He could barely dress himself in the morning, let alone a child, but that was beside the point. "I went back and forth and back and forth, going over all of the different scenarios in my head. Then a month or so ago, I went to Milwaukee to visit my family and my grandmother was rattling off about what I was supposed to do with my life. She said, 'Dane, all you have to do is find a nice girl and settle down with her. Then you will have a kid and make me a great-grandmother.' I was totally freaking out because of course, I was thinking, 'that may be happening sooner than you think grandma.'"

"So what happened?"

"I told Alexandra to call me when the baby was born," he said. "I waited and waited for what felt like years to hear from her. I didn't know what we were going to do if this baby was mine. She was not going to give it up for adoption so I guess I would have had to like send her money or some shit because I was totally not about to move to Guatemala."

I could see that Dane was not comfortable any longer. This poor, free spirited kid was loosing all of his spirit in front of my very eyes.

"Anyway," Dane continued, "I waited and waited for Alex's call but I never heard anything. So, I went on her facebook page and saw that she had baby picture's up. She must have had the baby and not had enough time to call me but enough time to post pictures on facebook."

I laughed, not knowing what else to do. Then asked: "Well, was it yours?"

"I couldn't look at the pictures," Dane said. "I asked my roommate to come over and look at the pictures for me because I was too afraid to look. She looked at the pictures and I asked her if the baby looked like me. She looked at the picture then looked at me and said she was pretty sure that the baby wasn't mine."

"How was she so sure that the baby wasn't yours?" I asked.

"The baby was black," he said as he laughed out loud. "The baby was black, and we are both white, so the baby could not possibly have been mine." He knocked back the remains of his margarita and continued, "nine months of freaking out for nothing. Who needs paternity tests when you have facebook?"

I laughed because it was the funniest thing I had ever heard. As I sat and stared at Dane, I realized I could have bore a child in my sobriety at this point. That is of course if I was a) a woman; and b) had not chain-smoked a pack and a half of cigarettes a day since I stopped drinking. It is always a pleasure to see my old drinking buddies because it not only reminds me of the crazy times I had as a drunk but reminds me how difficult it was to get to where I am today and how I would not jeopardize that for anything.

SPECIAL THANKS

So many people went into making this book possible. First of all, I need to thank Aimee, Tim, Anthony and William Brennan, who I owe at least a kidney each to at this point. You have done so much for me and you and have no idea how much I appreciate it. Thanks to Cameron Northey for your bad ass cover design and roommating skills. A very very very big thanks to Catherine Russell and everyone at the Snapple Theatre in New York for your support, for believing in me and for all of your help. You guys are the BEST. Super big shout outs to Luke Easley and Brian Knowles for helping me get sober and keeping me sober – without you, this book would have never been written.

There are so many amazing and supportive people in my life that I need to thank as well. Tom D'Angora for showing me that I could smile again and for of course, sharing the laughter and love. Evelyn Zilberman, Eric Saggese, Candace Holloway, Sally Schwab and every member of the Schwab family, Jason Cook, Michael Duling, Katelyn Sornik, Jennifer Tucker, Valerie Issembert, Krystal Roccaro, Damian Winters, Edward Donner, Emily Wilson (enter new married last name here), Maureen McDermott, Stephanie Buck (I don't know if you are really bisexual now, but I know you kissed a girl in high school so as far as I was concerned the jury was still out on that one), Jonathon Kearny, Kally Duling, Kathryn Owens for believing in me and taking that initial chance on me – even though it didn't work out ☹, Laura Hoffman-Watson, Lori Graham, Marla Schaffel, Maya Days, Meg Dougherty, Meghan Thornton, Britney Spears, Nick Blaemire, Justine Lore, Sara Vaccariello and Tim Rogers.

I was also like to thank my amazing siblings, niece and nephews. Your continued support and faith in me keeps me pretty inspired and makes me feel so incredibly loved. I would be nothing without all of you – Tony, Kim, Jamie, Kevin, Nikki, Finn, Devon, Jolie, Reed and Blake – I love you all so very much.

Most importantly I would like to thank my parents Pat and Keith. If you hadn't "done it twice" like my mother always says, I wouldn't be here. You have continued to support me in good times and bad and never ever gave up on me. Hopefully the sales of this book will buy us a house in Boca Raton and we can move there forever. It probably won't – so don't get your hopes up – but thanks anyway. Love you guys so much!!! Also props to my TV mom Susan Lucci. You just get better with age – don't you?

I would also like to thank any ex-boyfriends, second cousins or people in this book that I did not mention by name. Especially the citizens of New York and Washington D.C. for putting up with my terror and the good people down at the DCC. You know who you are – thanks for your help.